mind games

mind games

jeanne marie grunwell

HOUGHTON MIFFLIN COMPANY
BOSTON

Library of Congress Cataloging-in-Publication Data
Grunwell, Jeanne Marie.
Mind games / by Jeanne Marie Grunwell.
p. cm.
Sumary: Each of the six members of Mr. Ennis's Mad Science Club
presents a report of his or her experiences
working on a science fair project to investigate ESP,
which resulted in their winning the Maryland lottery.

ISBN 0-618-17672-1 (hardcover) ISBN 0-618-68947-8 (paperback)

[1. Science—Experiments—Fiction. 2. Extrasensory perception—Fiction.
3. Lotteries—Fiction. 4. Schools—Fiction. 5. Science—Exhibitions—Fiction.]
I. Title.
PZ7.G9338Mi   2003
[Fic]—dc21   2002010820

ISBN-13: 978-0618-17672-4 (hardcover)
ISBN-13: 978-0618-68947-7 (paperback)

Manufactured in the United States of America
HAD 10 9 8 7 6 5 4 3 2 1

FOR THE WONDERFUL TEACHERS I HAVE KNOWN

Acknowledgments

Thanks to my parents, who always taught me by example; Mr. Micklos, who introduced me to the scientific method; Mrs. Weingarten and Mr. Bennett, who made writing fun; the students and faculty of the MFA in Writing for Children program at Vermont College — especially Susan Fletcher, Randy Powell, Jane Resh Thomas, and Carolyn Coman; and thanks to Bonnie.

mind games

by
Benjamin D. Lloyd
Brandon Kelly
Marina Krenina
Ji Eun Oh
Claire Phelps
Kathleen Phelps

CLEARVIEW MIDDLE SCHOOL
GRADE 7

contents
by benjamin d. lloyd

---

[1] NOTE TO JUDGES: Paranormal Pursuits were originally intended for Mr. Ennis's edification and *not* for inclusion in the final project report. Please accept my apologies for their failure to conform to formatting specifications, which I delineated carefully for my fellow group members when they were apparently not listening. —BDL

ADDENDA TO CONTENTS

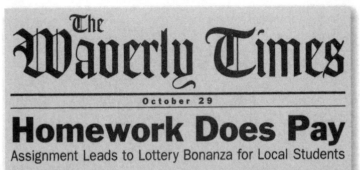

The Waverly Times

October 29

Homework Does Pay
Assignment Leads to Lottery Bonanza for Local Students

by Joanna Robles
Staff Writer

SIX Clearview Middle School seventh-graders are $500 richer after buying a Maryland State Lottery ticket this week in order to test a scientific hypothesis.

Benjamin Lloyd, 12, whose father purchased the winning ticket, declined to discuss details of the students' experiment, citing concerns of competition in the March 13 state science fair.

Principal Alice Mathews said she knew nothing of the unusual experiment under way in the seventh grade until her grandson informed her that he would no longer be complaining about excessive homework in James Ennis's science class. "What's more, he's shown an increased interest in math," Mathews added. "Word problems. For example, if he spends thirty dollars on CDs, does he have enough money left to buy new high-tops? I told him *I'd* buy him high-tops in exchange for information about their methodology. But he's not talking. And neither is Mr. Ennis."

"I can't explain it. I didn't even know the kids were playing the lottery," said Ennis, 34. "But I hope they'll cut me in on the profits if I contribute my fifty cents next time."

Ennis was as tight-lipped as his students regarding the nature of their experiment. "They plan to go public at the science fair. And that's about all I can say. But," he said, grinning, "I do predict a win."

experimenter comments
claire phelps

LAST NIGHT I WAS SUPPOSED TO READ OUR REPORT straight through and eliminate all typographical errors, missing commas, bad grammar, stupid-sounding parts, etc.

Considering that six of us worked on the same experiment and witnessed mostly the same events, I didn't think I would be too surprised by anything I read. Well, let's just say that my extreme cluelessness could be used as evidence against our hypothesis.

What I decided after reading our report was that six people worked on this project — six people who wrote what they wanted to write. Why should I change a word?

Of course I'm not thrilled about teachers and other people reading a lot of these things. I wish I never had to read them. But seeing yourself through other people's eyes is not such a bad thing. In a way, I guess that's what our project ended up being about.

I still feel we present a strong case for our hypothesis. But ultimately, the verdict rests with you, the reader. See what you think.

introduction
marina krenina

MR. ENNIS SAYS THAT THE INTRODUCTION IS SUP-
posed to be short, because this is not the interesting part of
the project. Of course I was given the short assignment.

This is very well, but it is not so short to explain how we
began.

I have recently learned the word *coincidence*. Certainly, that
is one way to describe all that has happened. But if you wish
to call it that, you have no need to read further in this report.

At our school, we have one class each week that we choose
for our own enjoyment. This is the only reason we go. It is
called a club. This is a strange thing for me, for we do nothing like this in Russia, where I come from.

The second week of school, in homeroom, we are asked
to choose the club we wish to join. At this time, my family
is in America only one month, and my English is not yet so
good. Of course I study some English in Russia, but I do not
know it as much as German or French. So when the teacher
talks fast, and all the students are also talking, I suddenly
understand only a few words, like *shut* and *up* and *detention*.

We have a paper to complete for the clubs, and I think this is a test. I cannot read so many words on this sheet. For example, there is the place to write my name, and there is the word *basketball*.

Next to me sits a boy named Ben Lloyd. Ben is very, very smart. Do not ask me how I know this, but I know. I see the answer he writes on his paper, and I think this must of course be the right answer to the test. So even though I understand it is a bad thing to do, I write the same answer on my club paper.

And that is how I came to be in Mr. Ennis's Mad Science Club.

At this time, I know only a few people at the school. Therefore, I think I will not know anyone who wants to study Mad Science besides Ben. But I am surprised at once. For I go to this club class, and here again is the girl with red hair.

On the first day of school I notice this girl immediately because of her thick braid, which is the color of the orange jam that my mother and I take every morning in our tea. I am admiring this beautiful hair tied with bright ribbons of green and gold, and all the while the girl is walking nearer to me. She is smiling. And suddenly she clutches my hair into her fist and draws it up to her nose. I am astonished. But then I think perhaps this is some American greeting which I have not yet observed. The girl shouts, "Cat fur!" I do not know what this means, but I see people stop in the hall to look at us, and I hurry away. I have not yet learned the meaning of this custom. It is a long while before I see it practiced by anyone else.

As I fear, on this day in Mr. Ennis's class the red-haired girl again takes my hair in her fist. But before she can make a nice sniff, her sister comes and begins to yell at her. I know it is her sister because of her red-blond ponytail and her voice, which resembles mine when I am angry with my younger sister, Lilia. However, it is difficult to know between these sisters which is the older. Their height is exactly the same shortness.

"Kathleen, don't do that!" the one sister shouts.

And Kathleen lets go of me, although not before she takes a tiny smell. "You smell so good," she tells me. "Like a pond in the woods." This makes me happy, because in Russia our dear dacha (summer home) was near a little lake in the forest. But I have not been there in two years, since the time we begin saving money to move to America. And I know my hair smells only of apricot and vanilla, which is the shampoo I use each morning, and probably too of Papa's cigarette smoke — the reason for me to use such nice shampoo.

When we are assembled in the classroom, we are at first five in addition to the teacher. Then is another surprise, for Brandon who is in my homeroom comes at the very last moment and sits next to me. Though he eats a Snickers bar plump with peanuts and sweet caramel, he seems to taste bitterness. I think I know why, for I have seen him mark the basketball space on his club paper. And I see he wears those shoes which make the nice squeak on the basketball court. I see this plainly, for his feet are on my chair.

At this time, Mr. Ennis introduces himself. Then he turns water into wine! And he turns it back!

Wine is not permitted in American public schools, and we are all very amazed, except for Brandon, who yawns. I see Ben and the girl named for the letter G leaning forward in their seats with much interest. But then Mr. Ennis says he never made wine. He shows us how his chemicals make the water change colors.

I do not watch the chemicals. I watch instead the lizard as it catches a cricket with its long tongue, and the turtles, three hiding very still among the rocks. I look in the third cage, but I see only a log and a dish that says *Alice*.

"Who is this Alice?" I whisper to Brandon.

"Alice?" he says. "My grandma."

Grandma, I think. I know this word. Dear Babushka, whose only fault is her snoring — and through many years of sharing a room, to this I have grown accustomed — is my grandma. Babushka, even if she were slim, would never fit in such a cage.

"I killed Alice," Kathleen says, quite cheerful as though she has just plucked a beautiful flower. Then she begins to cry. The sister produces a handful of tissues even before I notice a single tear.

"It is okay, Kathleen," I say. "Do not cry." Though in truth I cannot believe I am in the same room with the person who has killed the dear babushka of Brandon.

The sister whispers could I please try not to make Kathleen feel better. Or she will cry for an even greater time.

And then Brandon yawns. And Mr. Ennis talks some more about these chemicals. And Kathleen sobs and hiccups and finally is silent.

I look forward to returning to my ESL (English as a Second Language) class, where everything is simple — "How are you?" and "It is cloudy today." It is always cloudy today in Maryland.

Then I hear Mr. Ennis say *homework*.

"Dang, Mr. Ennis," Brandon says. "This is club. We're not supposed to have homework in club."

"That's right," G says.

I am thinking, how can I ever do this homework? I am not smart like these other people who have lifelong English.

Kathleen says, "I can't do the same homework as everybody else. I'm not smart like everybody else. I'm just stupid." She cries once more into her sister's tissues. I watch her sister take charge of these tissues — it is even more amazing than the water and the wine. Then Kathleen blows her nose, and I am *truly* amazed. Never have I heard the human nose make such a sound — not even Babushka's at night when she dreams her deepest dreams of home.

"You will do your homework together. Each of you will have your own part. Each of you will have something to contribute," Mr. Ennis says. "You are going to prepare a project for the school science fair in January."

Ben raises his hand immediately. "Can I work on anything

I want? I have a great idea. What about the county science fair? And the state? Will you be my sponsor?" He gasps for breath now, as though he has in fact been to basketball rather than Mad Science.

"Assuming you win the school science fair," Mr. Ennis says, "you will go to the county science fair in February. Assuming you place in the county science fair, you will go on to the state science fair in March. You are going to accomplish these things by researching a great mystery of science — *together*. And together, maybe you are going to solve it. Write down some ideas, and we will discuss them next week."

Ben puts his fists in the air, as though he is crossing the finish line after an Olympic race.

"The great mystery of science," G whispers to the tissue sister, "is Ben Lloyd."

I am surprised to discover I am a little bit interested in this project. I think of many questions I would like answered, such as which is better — Coke or Pepsi? And why must people grow old and die? And *why* is it always cloudy in Maryland?

When one week has passed and we again see Mr. Ennis, he asks us to write down one science mystery and hand it in without putting our name on the paper. I cannot write enough English for my idea, so I do nothing.

Mr. Ennis reads aloud from each paper.

"Does God exist?"

"Are dogs smarter than cats?"

"Hallucinogenic drugs and the blood-brain barrier."

"Solution of a seventeen-variable polynomial."

"Computation of the Hubble constant."

Mr. Ennis coughs. "I don't think all of us have turned in an idea," he says. "And I think one of us has turned in several."

We all look at Ben. He smiles like he knows he is important.

I raise my hand. "Mr. Ennis," I say, "I am not able to write my idea."

"That is fine, Marina," he says. "Can you tell us, then?"

I think Coke-Pepsi and cloudy weather do not sound so good after this Hubble constant. Therefore, I say, "Why must people grow old and die? Oh — but that is two questions." I feel myself growing flustered, and all the English words fly from my brain.

"How about dying without getting old?" Brandon kicks the desk with his nice basketball shoe.

"Claire didn't give you a question," Kathleen sings out, and she is glad to say something bad about her sister. This is very plain.

Claire's face turns pink and white, like a rabbit's.

"I know what her question would be," Kathleen says. "She wants to solve the mystery of how to make my . . . situation disappear."

Claire's face is now pinker and whiter than even a rabbit's. It is like a watermelon, the type with the white seeds. And her freckles are the dark seeds.

"But I don't want anyone experimenting on me," Kathleen says. "Anyhow, you can't fix it. So it wouldn't make a very good science project, would it?"

I think this will be another time for the tissues, but I am wrong.

"Kathleen, you have made an excellent point," Mr. Ennis says, and Claire pats her on the shoulder.

Kathleen beams, showing many straight teeth.

"If you are going to solve a scientific problem, you must be able to carry out an *experiment*. The Hubble constant? Seventeen-variable polynomials? Maybe someday when you are astrophysicists and mathematicians. For now, let's think realistically of what we can do. And please — no hallucinogenic drugs, either, regardless of their effect on the blood-brain barrier. The school board might frown on that kind of experiment."

Ben frowns on Mr. Ennis. "Geez," he says, "I was kidding. Doesn't anybody have a sense of humor around here?" The bell rings. Ben lifts his giant backpack onto his shoulders. "I hate this class," he murmurs as he races from the room. No one seems to hear him but I.

Brandon shakes his head. "Homework. Reading. I knew I was gonna hate this class."

"Me, too," says G.

"Us, too," say Kathleen and Claire.

"I guess we're all on the same wavelength," G says.

I have said nothing. Therefore, I do not know if G feels my opinion does not matter, or rather if she knows my opinion even though I do not speak. But I, too, am on the same wavelength. Now that I know what this means, I can say it for certain.

And that is when it happens.

"That's it!" G shouts. "I've got a great idea for our experiment!"

The next week, Mr. Ennis writes the subject of our experiment in big letters on the chalkboard. I later discover that we are solving the great mystery of ESP. And what this is, I have then not the least idea.

paranormal pursuits: astrology
ji eun oh

Task: Examine my horoscope for five days. Record what really happens. Count how many things come true (1 point per correct prediction).

Amendment: Also count how many things are too vague to count (0 points each).

Purpose: To see whether astrology can accurately predict the future.

My parents subscribe to the *Wall Street Journal*. It doesn't have a horoscope section, which is okay, because my parents are Presbyterian and therefore anti-horoscope. However, we do receive the *Waverly Times*. My parents have no choice because, horoscope or not, this paper is delivered free every week.

Ben Lloyd says the horoscope writer for the *Waverly Times* isn't even a professional astrologer but a plain old reporter disguising her name out of embarrassment. As editor of the school newspaper, I tried not to take "plain old reporter" as an insult. I asked Ben how he knew this information, and that was the last I heard from him on the subject.

Because I was forced to use a weekly paper, evaluating five horoscopes took much longer than five days. (Sorry, Mr. Ennis.) Here are the results:

Excerpts from "Sun Signs" by Cassidy Richards
The *Waverly Times* (Aries section)

October 8 *Persist in your favorite pursuits despite obstacles that may present themselves.*[1] *Focus on group work.*[2] *Make new friends, but keep the old.*[3]

ANALYSIS (10/15):

1. Shopping and socializing are my favorite pursuits, according to my parents. They are already expert obstacles to my doing anything fun, but I am experter at getting around them. Another thing I like to do, I guess, is sing. However, I quit the church choir a few weeks ago—and I wouldn't want to persist, no matter what this horoscope says. I *am* still in the choir at school, and we have auditions this Monday for the winter concert. I am planning on getting a solo (assuming God does not punish me for reading this horoscope and maybe even believing it). PREDICTION COR-RECT? ½ point.

2. Since you are reading this, you will see that I am

focused on my Mad Science "group work." PREDICTION
CORRECT? 1 point.

3. Friends are very important to me. I made lots of new
ones when we started middle school last year. Claire, unfortunately, did not. But that's okay. She's still my friend. In
terms of making friends this year, I've only met two new
people — Brandon and Marina. Brandon seems to know one
sentence, which is *I don't care.* Marina knows a few more,
but they all seem to be about food and the weather. Therefore, I'm not sensing good friendship material here. PRE-
DICTION CORRECT? ½ point.

> October 15   *Romantic prospects are encouraging.*[1] *You will
> receive good news regarding a worrisome situation.*[2] *In your
> busy state of life, friendships may suffer.*[3]

ANALYSIS (10/22):

1. Romance? Yeah, right. My parents won't even let me
date until I'm sixteen. I'm tempted to give negative points
for this one. PREDICTION CORRECT? 0 points.

2. If this counts, I did get that choir solo — not that I was
so worried. I usually try to leave the freak-outs to people
like my parents and Claire. So the only thing really bothering me right now is this week's prediction #3. PREDIC-
TION CORRECT? ½ point (I guess).

3. My friendships are doing pretty well, I have to say.
Therefore, I want to believe very much that this prediction
deserves: PREDICTION CORRECT? 0 points.

And it had better not have anything to do with Claire.

Also of note — October 15 was Claire's birthday (and her sister, Kathleen's). The entry for "If today is your birthday" read as follows:

Your day begins on a high note. Brisk exercise will do wonders for your constitution. You will clear a major hurdle this week. Sit back, relax, and enjoy the show.

ANALYSIS:

In choir (second period), Kathleen croaked on a high A and cried into the piano; after exercise (but not hurdles) in P.E., she threw up chocolate cake on the track; she enjoyed the clown at her party on Saturday, although she did not enjoy my being invited. (She did enjoy my arriving late due to Katie Baird's party being on the same day.) Furthermore, she neither sat nor relaxed. Except when she is petting her dog, I have never seen Kathleen relax.

On the other hand, Claire sings alto when she sings at all (hardly ever), but she did start first period on a high note by getting a 92 on the algebra test everybody else (including me) failed; she had no bad effects from brisk exercise in P.E., and she did not enjoy the clown show so much. But she stayed relaxed even when Kathleen blew out all the candles and stole her birthday wish; I guess she's used to that (and to the spit on her cake) after all these years.

PREDICTION CORRECT? This is too complicated to score in my opinion, but if the same horoscope is supposed to apply to Claire and Kathleen (not to mention Katie Baird), that's enough evidence to persuade me that astrology is totally inaccurate.

> October 22   *Cash in on your popularity. Keep your head on your shoulders when confronted with a tricky situation. Speak your mind — you will be appreciated for it.*

ANALYSIS (10/29):
I cashed in — we won the lottery. As for the rest of the prediction, it doesn't matter since I will not be doing any further work on this project.

research
benjamin d. lloyd

FOR THE PURPOSE OF THIS PROJECT, I HAVE READ SIX books about parapsychology, two books about science fair projects (see Sources), and various other materials too numerous to list.

So that you might try to understand the subject of my discussion, I am providing you with the following:

DEFINITIONS

Clairvoyance: Uncanny knowledge of other living things and/or events that is not gained through telepathy (see below).

ESP (Extra-Sensory Perception): The process of accumulating knowledge that cannot be gained by the use of our five known senses (such as why this topic was chosen for our science project).

Paranormal: Phenomena outside the realm of "normal" experience.

Parapsychology: The (supposedly) scientific study of ESP.

Psychokinesis (P.K.): The influence of the human mind on inanimate objects.

Telepathy: The ability to know another person's thoughts.

EVALUATION

A comprehensive review of (so-called) scientific literature pertaining to these topics reveals that conclusive results have not been achieved in any previous study conducted under valid testing conditions. Demonstrated instances of ESP have not been readily reproduced under controlled observation. Ever.[1] Furthermore, anecdotal evidence of supernatural occurrences thus far is totally insufficient to convince a self-respecting scientist that science cannot satisfactorily explain the world around us. Indeed, the "fortunetellers" my mother used to hire at her holiday parties routinely made such predictions as a long and happy marriage for my parents and great scientific achievements for me. While we still await the verdict on my scientific accomplishments, the assertion regarding my parents' marriage proves that ESP is certainly not an exact science — and probably not a science at all.

One more noteworthy thing. Claire and Kathleen Phelps, members of our investigative team, are homozygous twins.[2] Twin studies are mentioned several times in parapsychol-

---

[1] Except in those cases of fraud, of course, which appears rampant in this field of research.

[2] I.e., identical (although this is a highly misleading term when it comes to Claire and Kathleen).

ogy literature, so I felt this area warranted further investigation on my part.

In the ongoing debate of nature versus nurture, it is thought that identical twins who were separated at birth and raised in different families can provide good evidence about which is more important — genes or upbringing.[3]

I read several interesting cases about twins who had never known each other before meeting during the study, only to discover that they'd each married a woman named Anna, had a child named Sam, and liked to eat a bowl of butter pecan ice cream with pretzels while watching *I Love Lucy* before bed.[4]

After examining the literature, I suggested to my research team that perhaps nature versus nurture would make a more interesting topic for our project. I am very interested, for example, to know whether my science aptitude comes from my inheritance of my father's astrophysicist genes or is instead a result of having *Scientific Weekly* read aloud to me at age four. Brandon dismissed this idea by saying that I'm destined to be a science geek either way, and who cares why? I nobly refrained from pointing out that he's destined to be a science zero either way, and who cares why? Due to a general lack of interest on the part of my

---

[3] Identical twins provide good evidence because they have identical genes. Therefore, if they were raised in different families, their degree of similarity as adults is due totally to their genetic makeup.

[4] This is a made-up story, but you get the idea. It is a fairly typical example.

fellow group members, I was forced to abandon once again a potentially fascinating topic. But I remain curious. After all, my mother, who was never a geek and in fact was once a cheerleader, got a D in high school chemistry and during her days as an aspiring magazine writer was an avid reader of such periodicals as *Cosmopolitan* and *Glamour*. Half of my genes are hers. Is this not strange?

Of course, Claire and Kathleen have the exact same genes, and Claire is in honors classes[5] while Kathleen is in special ed. One wonders where brain damage counts in nature versus nurture.

Besides shedding light on nature versus nurture, the twin studies also highlighted several "psychic" events involving twins who were separated at birth. For example, one woman had an attack of appendicitis. Her sister was rushed to the hospital at the same time with a sharp pain in her side, but the doctors could find nothing wrong with her. At the time, neither woman knew she had a twin.

Is this convincing proof of ESP? No. Is it semiconvincing proof of ESP? No, because ESP is not the only possible explanation of these events. For example, the second twin's pain may not have been caused by the first twin's attack of appendicitis. It may have been caused by the bad lasagna she ate the night before.[6]

---

[5] That's a step below GT — Gifted and Talented — which I'm in.

[6] Having cooked several such unpalatable meals since my mother moved out, I can attest that this pain is quite intense.

As I formulated a plan for the design of our experiment, I decided to approach Kathleen and Claire for any recollections of ESP-type phenomena that they might have experienced. My question was answered immediately and enthusiastically by Kathleen, who recounted an incident in kindergarten in which she was crushed because she was denied access to someone's hair for sniffing purposes.[7] Claire, knowing instinctively that Kathleen was upset, came hurrying from another classroom to comfort her twin. That Claire may have heard her bloodcurdling shriek did not, apparently, enter into Kathleen's consideration.[8]

Kathleen also mentioned various incidents involving a pig from her family's small farm, a snake, and someone named Sunshine.[9] My suggestion of an experiment to verify Kathleen's claims was vetoed, leading me to further doubt the reliability of her report. That is just as well, because such an experiment would be nightmarish. I am allergic to furry animals, I would find it difficult to obtain a live pig, and the snake is not available for testing, as it was inadvertently murdered by Kathleen.[10]

Marina subsequently contributed a tale about Mr. Ennis

---

[7] This is a quirky behavior that Kathleen is known to perpetrate to this day.

[8] As the owner of the hair in question, I was so traumatized as to nearly become a kindergarten dropout, except that my mother refused to let my father home-school me. Too bad. I could be in college now.

[9] Determined after extensive questioning to be a dog.

[10] Do not mention this incident to her. She will cry.

and wine (?), which I was unable to comprehend due to her poor command of the English language and pronunciation thereof. Claire boasted of an astounding history of success at Pictionary when partnered with Ji, who had been known to guess the subject of a drawing before Claire even put her pen to paper. During this conversation, Brandon hastily exited the room for unknown reasons. Mr. Ennis followed him, and neither returned for the remainder of the class period. Therefore, I was unable to obtain their input.

The only premonition I personally have ever had[11] was that my parents would get a divorce. That had nothing to do with psychic phenomena and everything to do with life experience — ten years' worth.

Given little material to work with from my research partners, I thus began researching experimental techniques so that we might improve upon the findings of our hapless parapsychology researchers.

At this time, Mr. Ennis requested documentation of the progress made in our research pursuits. As none had yet occurred, he suggested we might wish to proceed in a speedier fashion.

He then asked to see a report from each of us before the end of October.

Since I was the only individual actually working on the project at this time, I asked Mr. Ennis whether I could pursue my Hubble investigation instead. He encouraged me

---

[11] Besides winning the lottery — see below.

to pursue any topic I wished; however, he made it clear that our group experiment must be complete before he would allow me to enter an individual project in the science fair under his sponsorship.

As my fellow group members failed to grasp the exciting possibilities of the Hubble constant, I realized it was incumbent on me to assume a leadership role and prod them into some sort of action. In an attempt to interest them in the investigation — any investigation — I suggested the Paranormal Pursuits projects to be found throughout this document.

As we devised ideas for our individual Paranormal Pursuits, I also enlisted help from the group in collecting materials for our legitimate parapsychology experiment. The complete list turned out to be as follows:

MATERIALS
1) One black pen (which will not bleed)
2) 5" × 7" index cards (25)
3) One shoebox
4) One pair of dice
5) One plastic cup

To this, we later added:

6) One dictionary
7) Drawing paper
8) Lottery tickets

Traditional ESP testing cards (aka Zener cards) were made using the black pen and index cards. Claire, known since first grade for her neatness, made five of each of the following designs: *plus*, *circle*, *box*, *star*, and *wavy lines* (see cards, display table).

From here, we embarked on our first attempts to discern evidence of the paranormal in the world around us.

EXHIBIT C

paranormal pursuits:
telepathy
claire phelps

IF I WERE EVER GOING TO TRY TO READ SOMEONE'S mind, I didn't think it would be my twin sister's. The person I know better than anybody is Ji. At least, I used to. But by the time we decided to do this ESP project, I was surprised that she thought we were on the same wavelength anymore — about anything.

Now that Ji has so many new friends, I spend a lot of time wondering what she wants to do with me. When I ask her, she says I'm crazy to worry that things have changed. But her not admitting it to me — that's definitely part of the change.

What is our friendship about to her? If I could read her mind, that's what I'd want to know.

But I can't do it. I've tried and tried. That's when Ben pointed out to me that I've tried and tried with Ji, and who knows how long we'll be friends? With Kathleen, who's my sister for life, I've never tried.

• • •

I am older than Kathleen by four minutes, although sometimes it seems like four years. My father held me during those four minutes, and my mother gave me a name — Claire Catherine, after her two favorite saints.

The first thing I did in this world was to almost kill my sister (not very saintlike) by using all our oxygen when we were being born. The first thing Kathleen did was shut her mouth tight and not breathe and not cry. She has since made up for this many times over.

Kathleen didn't get her name until the third day, when everybody was sure she was going to live. I was already home from the hospital then, and Aunt Lynn came to take care of me. Aunt Lynn says I cried the whole time. She says I couldn't bear to be separated from my sister.

So when Ben started talking about research on twins separated at birth, I thought about Kathleen and me and all the things between us ever since the day we were born.

I tried to understand how these twins who had never met each other in their whole lives could be closer than me and Kathleen. How could they share butter pecan ice cream across 2,000 miles when Kathleen and I can't even share a birthday cake? How could they laugh at the same jokes when I've heard Kathleen's chicken crossing the road every day since kindergarten and never laughed once? How could they feel each other's gut-wrenching pain (literally) when Kathleen's can only make me a little bit numb?

And I thought, *How come I can't read her mind when she's never out of my thoughts for one minute?*

I definitely feel that being Kathleen's twin qualifies as a paranormal experience. I might have chosen this topic for my Paranormal Pursuit, but that would take a whole book. Sorry, Mr. Ennis, but we're not getting a grade in this class.

Ji is an only child, and she says she never feels lonely. Meanwhile, I am a twin, and sometimes I feel like the loneliest person in the world. Well, maybe not quite. Maybe that's one area where Kathleen and I are pretty equal.

I'd never thought about trying to get inside Kathleen's head before. First of all, the idea's kind of scary. And second, why should I? I already know when Kathleen's going to need a tissue even before she starts crying; I know when she's going to need a scolding even before she does something wrong; I know when she's going to sing "On Eagle's Wings" when the rest of the congregation is singing "Amazing Grace," or hug Mr. Ennis when he's trying to teach a lesson. I know when she's going to feed my homework to the pig or let the dog chew my cleats. But I know these things from experience, not ESP. And knowing doesn't help me prevent any of them from happening. Besides, it's not the same as understanding why she has to be the center of attention — always.

Whatever I give her — praise, time, all my Halloween candy every year — it's never what she wants; it's never enough. How could it be?

Kathleen takes, and she takes, and, as much as I want to make up for what I took from her, how could I ever?

Sometimes she tells people — strangers in church — that I hit her.

Once — I hit her *once* when we were four. She hit me first. Because I ate the last Special Dark out of the Hershey's Miniatures bag.

Mom said I knew Special Dark was Kathleen's favorite. It wasn't *my* favorite. I should have saved it for her, I should have been more understanding, I certainly shouldn't have hit her back. I should have been a better sister.

That day I sat in the corner and listened to Kathleen laugh and play and chase after the puppy the way she usually chased after me. I can still taste that memory — chocolate and tears that stayed bitter on the back of my tongue for a long, long time.

Normal sisters fight, but we don't — not anymore. Now I swallow everything and let her do the crying for both of us.

Ben gave me an article to read about twin girls. They're conjoined twins, attached at the chest. They share the same heart. They can never be apart from each other — never, as long as they live. Each of them has one leg, and if they want to walk, they have to use both their legs together. That means they always have to agree where they want to go.

Sometimes I feel as though Kathleen and I are tied together like that, ever since our umbilical cords got tangled before we were born. And — just like then — she's trying to go one way, and I'm trying to go the other.

Today's our birthday, and I hate thinking of one more

year growing between us, pushing that big space into something even bigger.

When Kathleen blows out all our birthday candles every year, does she understand the wish I'd make if she gave me the chance? Does she understand she's taking that away from both of us?

I don't know. I don't have ESP.

I'm sorry to say that my telepathy project isn't complete, Mr. Ennis. It's just starting. I have a feeling it might take another seventy years before I can give you any conclusive results. Before I can say that I understand Kathleen. I apologize for missing the deadline, but I have a feeling you understand.

problem

kathleen "kat" phelps

(as told to Whitney Phelps, mother*)

MY ONE PROBLEM IS ALICE. SHE'S — WELL, SHE WAS
— a snake. Mr. Ennis's milk snake, but she didn't eat milk.
Just mice and small reptiles. She was a present from our
principal, Mrs. Mathews, for Mr. Ennis's classroom. That's
why he named her Alice. After Mrs. Mathews.

Mr. Ennis is my homeroom teacher. He's this very nice
man with glasses. He says hi to me and listens when I talk
to him, and he smells very good. He doesn't wear cologne
or aftershave. I think it's his deodorant. Spring Fresh scent.

I'm glad I'm in Mr. Ennis's homeroom. The only bad part
is that they do homerooms by the alphabet. That means my
sister Claire is there. We don't usually have classes together,
except homeroom and P.E. and special stuff like club. We
don't like to very much, either.

---

*NOTE: The opinions contained herein are those of the writer and
do not reflect in the least those of the transcriptionist!

36

My problem started on club-picking day. See, I wanted to be in the WCTV club. That's the Clearview News Channel. I wanted to read the news on TV like Diane Sawyer. She's famous. I even dreamed about it the night before. I was a famous anchorperson on TV like Diane Sawyer.

But Claire doesn't like me getting attention. She always tries to put a stop to it. She wouldn't like me to pick that club, not one little bit. I even thought she might change my club paper when I wasn't looking. I wouldn't put it past her.

So on club-picking day, I tried to sit far away from Claire. Only, away from Claire happened to be near the snake cage. I usually try to avoid the snake cage area because it makes me so sad.

Alice was a nice snake — charming. Ha — charming snake. That's funny, isn't it?

Here's another good one. What did one strawberry say to the other? If you hadn't been so fresh, we wouldn't have gotten into this jam.

Alice had shiny eyes. And nice skin, for a snake. But she looked sad. Sad and smushed.

"Let me out!" it seemed like she was saying. "I don't belong here."

I knew how she felt. Exactly precisely.

But I couldn't help her. I told her I couldn't. It was against the rules to let her out. Mr. Ennis said.

But Alice didn't take no for an answer. No, she didn't. She slithered off her log and looked me in the eye. RIGHT IN THE EYE.

Old Claire was watching me with her beady eyes. And

that friend of hers, Ji Oh, too. Ji tries to act like she's my friend, but I'm not stupid. She treats me like a baby, just like Claire.

I stood up and bent over the cage so Claire couldn't see everything I was doing. Then I lifted up the lid to Alice's cage. I thought I could just scratch her between the eyes the way Sunshine likes.

"It's okay," I whispered to Alice. "Don't be afraid."

Alice hugged me. She hugged me and kissed me and sniffed my hair with her tongue. Snakes are cold-blooded, but she was real warm.

I let her crawl around and stretch a little, so she could unsmush. She's the one who decided to crawl out the window. She wanted to be free. I thought it would be the best thing for her.

That's when we got caught, me and Alice.

Ji tried to pull Alice back through the window. But Alice was too slippery for her. Then Ji started crying that Alice bit her. It was just a little tongue lick, though. Ji is such a baby.

I was real happy for Alice, that she was free. I was happy for a little while, because I didn't know yet.

I didn't know a milk snake isn't made to live in Maryland in the woods in the wintertime. Or even the fall. That's why Alice is dead and gone. It hurts me that it happened. But I didn't mean to let her die. Don't listen to what other people say.

Claire kept asking me why did I let Alice go out the window. I started breathing real hard and hyperventilating like. I couldn't say anything. She got real mad because I wouldn't answer her question.

That's when Mr. Ennis sent us all to the office — me and Claire and Ji. Ji put cold water on her finger. Claire made me breathe into a paper bag that smelled like McDonald's french fries. Mrs. Mathews called my mother to say I killed her snake that was named after her. That's when the WCTV club got filled up. The death of the snake was their first main story. But I never thought I'd get on TV that way.

So that's how we ended up in Mr. Ennis's Mad Science Club. Mr. Ennis signed us up without asking us. That's okay. But why he'd want to spend more time than he has to with Claire and Ji is a big mystery to me.

Mad Science isn't as bad as it could be. For one thing, there's this girl named Marina. She has the nicest-smelling, prettiest hair. It's thick and curly and black. But her eyes are blue — just like a cat's. I like cats. I would like to be called Kat, but nobody ever remembers to. Except Marina. Marina lets me smell her hair when Claire isn't looking. It makes me feel all warm and fuzzy inside.

Another good thing is that our project is about ESP. Nobody knows this, but I've always thought I have ESP. Like how I dreamed about Diane Sawyer, and then my name got to be on the first WCTV show. Also, I can always tell what my dog, Sunshine, is thinking. Like when she stands by the cupboard and whines, and Mom thinks she wants a dog biscuit and Claire thinks Kibbles 'n Bits, but I know she's asking for a spoonful of peanut butter. I'm good to Sunshine, and she's good to me. She always knows when I'm sad. Then she'll curl up next to me and lay her chin across my face and kiss me so that it tickles and I have to laugh. Claire says tears taste good because they're salty and that's why Sunshine pays attention to me. But Claire's just jealous because Sunshine likes me best.

Claire thinks she can read my mind, but she can't. I can read hers, though. I know she wishes she didn't have a dumb old twin like me.

How's that for a problem?

Oh, about the science fair problem. ESP.

Is there ESP? That's the problem. It's not a very hard one, is it? We solve lots harder ones in special ed. Every single day.

paranormal pursuits:
clairvoyance
benjamin d. lloyd

TASK: Each time the phone rings, guess the name of the person who is calling. Count the number of correct guesses.

PURPOSE: To document evidence of clairvoyance if it should happen to appear.

Date	Time	Prediction	Caller
10/8	7:22 P.M.	Mom	Dad
10/9	8:05 P.M.	Mom	Dad
10/11	7:49 P.M.	Dad	Cassidy Robles (half sister)
10/11	7:52 P.M.	Dad	Mom
10/12	8:14 P.M.	Dad	Dad
10/12	10:33 P.M.	Nana (Mrs. Mary Lamb)	Nana
10/14	7:53 P.M.	Dad	Brandon Kelly
10/14	7:57 P.M.	Brandon	Brandon
10/14	7:59 P.M.	Dad	Dad
10/17	10:00 A.M.	Mom	Telemarketer
10/17	10:30 A.M.	Mom	Rick Robles (Mom's husband)
10/19	8:00 P.M.	Mom	Claire Phelps
10/21	8:00 P.M.	Claire	Claire
10/23	10:00 P.M.	Claire	Claire
10/25	7:00 P.M.	Dad	Claire
10/27	7:55 P.M.	Brandon	Brandon
10/27	7:57 P.M.	Mom	Marina Krenina
10/27	7:59 P.M.	Mom	Claire
10/27	8:32 P.M.	Mom	Mom

To say he would be home late.

To say he would be home late.

Was playing with the phone and hit autodial.

To apologize for the autodial.

Finally got one right!

Has difficulty calculating the time difference from Arizona (partly due to senility, but also daylight-savings time).

To see if we'd won the lottery (the drawing does not take place until 7:56 P.M.).

To say we hadn't won the lottery.

To ask why the line was busy and what I wanted on my pizza.

Participated in cereal survey.

Pertaining to arrangements for our weekend visitation.

To ask about a homework assignment.

Regarding the Halloween dance.

Pertaining to events at the Halloween dance.

I don't know why.

To say we'd won the lottery.

To say we'd won the lottery.

To say we'd won the lottery.

A work-related question.

Total Correct: 8 out of 19 (42.1 percent)

Explanation and Analysis: I would not admit this except for the sake of science, but here goes. After my mother moved out, I would on occasion focus on the phone and will it to ring.

I remember in elementary school how anxious Mom felt that my friends should call me. That my friends should *exist*. I'm afraid I proved a terrible disappointment to her in this regard.

Mom now has a female infant who will assuredly satisfy her needs for unexceptional, socially interactive offspring. Her interest in my life has waned accordingly.

While my brain is powerful, it cannot do the impossible — it cannot make my mom call me when she does not want to. This fact is clearly documented above.

I am accustomed to people not wanting to talk to me, and that is perfectly acceptable. It has afforded me tremendous opportunities to focus on my scientific pursuits, uninterrupted and without distraction.

However, I began to be distracted by the phone eighteen months ago, when the probability approached 90 percent that a given caller would be Rick Robles. I have remained distracted throughout Mom's leaving us and marrying Rick Robles and causing the probability to approach 0 percent that our phone would ever ring again.

This has changed in the month of October, when I have received an unprecedented nine calls from classmates and Mom has demonstrated a renewed interest in my life as of the twenty-seventh. Due to the superficial nature of her concern, I will not tell her of my sudden popularity.[1] At any rate, it would be unwise to get one's hopes up. The callers will go away. So will my mom. One does not need paranormal powers to know these things.

---

[1] Although there was a time when she would have perceived this as thrilling news.

hypothesis
brandon kelly

THE PROBLEM IS, IS THERE ESP?

We took a vote to figure out what our hypothesis would be. It was three to three. Me and Marina and Kathleen, we said yes. Claire and Ji and Benjamin D. Lloyd, they said no.

Since Kathleen is retarded and Marina doesn't speak English and my grandma says I don't use the sense the good Lord gave me, we didn't figure it was worth bothering to have a tiebreaker.

But Claire said we should be fair. So she got dice, and I called it even, and she rolled. Maybe it was an intuition on my end, I don't know, but she threw a two and our side won.

So we had our hypothesis. But Mr. Ennis said we had to have a reason for our hypothesis — more than just a two of dice, or whatever you want to call it.

I told him I'd take care of the reason.

To tell you the truth, I don't care too much for this whole Mad Science deal. For one thing, I signed up for the basketball club. I bet I'm the only person in the whole school who didn't get in the club they signed up for. I'm also the only person in the school who's grandma is the principal. Coincidence? I don't think so.

For another thing, ESP is just about the dumbest subject we could've picked for a project. Benjamin D. Lloyd would've done all the work for us if we'd played it right. But no, we had to go and vote for the only experiment he *didn't* want to do.

Personally, I'd like to have seen us do bread mold. Just to see the look on Grandma's face. She's against dirt, dust, and green things growing in the refrigerator. She's not too used to having a boy in the house yet.

Mr. Ennis, he's cool. He gives me tips sometimes on how to handle Grandma. For example, she's particular about things like grammar. I admit my grammar needs some work. But Grandma needs a little vocabulary help, too. Like when I said "hang time," she thought I meant on the corner of Fayette and Paca. And when I said "run and gun," she about had a heart attack. That's when Mr. Ennis took us both to see a Wizards game. It helped some.

I thought Mr. Ennis might talk to Grandma about getting me in the basketball club. Talk to her yourself, he said. Like I didn't try that already. Grandma said I could play winter ball and rec league and summer league, too. But school is for learning. And I need science help. Besides, I like spending time with Mr. Ennis, don't I?

It wasn't Mr. Ennis I was worried about. It was those other five people who *wanted* to study science in their free time.

• • •

I have a hypothesis, I told Mr. Ennis. I have a hypothesis that this science club is gonna suck.

Prove it, he said to me.

I didn't care to bother.

Like I said, ESP is about the worst topic we could've picked for a project. Especially for me.

See, my little brother is named after a prophet in the Bible. Hosea. I think Ma must've had ESP when she named him, because he's just like that. Always thinking he knows what he doesn't have any business knowing.

When Ma told him about Santa and the Easter Bunny, he didn't believe her. They're not real, he said to her. Oh, honey, but they are, Ma said.

Finally Hosea went and found my baby teeth in Ma's jewelry box. He was like four years old then. Maybe even littler. Grandma took him to the library, and he asked for a book about the Tooth Fairy. Wanted to do research, he said.

Ain't no such thing as the Tooth Fairy, he told me that night. No Santa or the Easter Bunny, neither.

Now I guess I really knew before he told me. But it still wasn't any of his business to say it out loud. If he told Michael, I said I was going to beat him up good. For once he kept his big mouth shut.

Hosea and Michael used to sleep in the same bed when we lived in the old row house on Greenmount. Hosea was real restless. Always talking and kicking and pushing Michael out of bed in the middle of the night. Michael wouldn't even cry. He'd just sleep right there on the floor. He can sleep through anything.

Michael slept through it that night Hosea sat up in bed, screaming about Ma dying. Ma's dead, Ma's dead!

I jumped up so fast, I whacked my head on the basketball hoop Ma stuck up over my bed.

Darius — that's Hosea and Michael's dad — he went in and shushed him. Ma was at work, he said. On the late shift at Mercy Hospital.

Hosea kept on crying. Couldn't Darius go out and find Ma? Make sure she was okay? I felt the hair stand up on my arms. I felt like something was really, really wrong. Because we all knew how Hosea could feel things and know things he shouldn't be able to.

Then we heard these footsteps in the hallway, real soft. I about jumped a mile.

It was Ma.

We didn't hear you come in, Darius said. That's when I saw his hand up by his waist like he was gonna pull his gun. But he was wearing his boxers, of course, so the gun was locked away in the secret hiding place. I thought, Darius is a cop and he was scared, too.

Ma said she was trying to be quiet so she wouldn't wake us up. She took out a tissue from her pocket — a good nurse is always prepared — and wiped Hosea's nose. He kept sniffling and snotting all over her uniform.

Ma rocked Hosea so he'd go back to sleep and give the rest of us some peace. But he wouldn't. He said he was afraid he'd have the same dream over again. The dream that she was dead.

The next day we went to Kim's market and it got robbed.

Mr. Kim handed over all the money from the register. Then the robber ran away, and Mr. Kim chased after him. Next thing I knew a bullet came right through the glass, went flying by my head. Busted open a jar of pickles on the shelf next to me. Kosher dills. Ma always hated pickles, but she kissed all that pickle juice off my forehead.

That's when Darius said he was moving us out of the city. We didn't want to go, none of us. But he got us a nice little house in Woodlawn. Just like it sounds, with a little lawn in the front, a little woods in the back. Little basketball court in the driveway.

It wasn't so different from the city. Except Ma learned to drive so she wouldn't have to change buses fourteen different times to get to work. They signed up Hosea for a soccer league where he could put his kicking foot to good use. Michael got his own bed and his own room. As for me — my life didn't change too much. Not till the day somebody hit Ma's car on the JFX and she died at Mercy Hospital where she worked.

Obviously, I don't live in Woodlawn no more. I live in boring old Waverly with my grandma. You could take the bus for a hundred stops and never make it to the city. The bus doesn't even come way out here.

Darius doesn't have any obligation or anything since he's not my real dad, but he probably would've kept me if I acted respectful. A cop's son can't be in trouble for shoplifting and stuff, he kept on saying. I understand why Darius was mad. He said he wanted to help me, but he didn't know what to do. He said I was almost a teenager and needed to learn some rules, some respect. If anyone could teach me about tough love, it was Grandma.

Grandma said she got where I was coming from, but it wasn't Darius's fault, or Hosea's, that Ma's dead. I know it wasn't. But I can't help thinking, Darius is the one who moved us out to Woodlawn, made Ma get that beat-up old car. And if it wasn't for Hosea making us all so jittery with that dream, we'd still live in the city.

Ma died this past January 13. That's one year to the day after Hosea had his dream. To the day.

And that's why it's my hypothesis that there is such a thing as ESP.

paranormal pursuits:
out-of-body experiences
kathleen phelps

(as told to James Ennis, teacher)

I LIKE TO IMAGINE WHAT IT WOULD BE LIKE TO BE somebody else. Well, not somebody, exactly. I would like to be a dog. Dogs are smarter than most people think. But even with having brain damage, I'm smarter than a dog. Dogs are just more huggable and kissable and lovable. Especially Sunshine.

Sometimes I think I'd like to switch places with Sunshine. She has red hair like mine. She likes to share Popsicles, and she sings with me in the shower. We're like real sisters.

Still, there are some good parts about being human, like being able to sing words and ride roller coasters and laugh at a clown. It is also good to live longer than ten or twelve years.

That's why I thought it would be nice to be Sunshine for just a minute. To get away from being me and be Sunshine instead.

I started practicing at night when I was sleepy. I would put my hand on Sunshine's head and feel her nose go from wet to hot. I would feel her whiskers tickle under my fingers and her eyelids flicker so the whites showed under her red eyelashes. Then I would bury my face in her fur and imagine her dream. Myself in her dream.

Pretty soon, I could wag my tail. I could smell Penny the barn cat from inside my bedroom. And see how the moonlight looked different, with new colors in every single thing—my Beauty and the Beast curtains and the freckles on my hands and the sheep I would count when my eyes were closed. And I could see Claire in the new light, too, with the moon shining on her hair so it looked as sparkly green as her eyes.

It was a long time ago when I started dreaming with Sunshine, maybe even before special ed. But I never told anybody about it until now. You know Claire would just say it was dumb and weird. I finally told because of the science project.

I don't think Ben believed me, but he said if it did really happen with Sunshine, it's called an out-of-body experience, which is a pair of normal [sic] phenomenon. I knew it. I *knew* it was normal. I guess it's called a pair because it's both of us—me and Sunshine.

Ben says we need to do an experiment on me and Sunshine so we can have evidence that this out-of-body thing happens. I don't know what he's talking about. It happens. Would I make up something like that?

So I said no to the experiment. Anyhow, how was he planning to do it? I don't think you can prove what's in a person's dreams, or even a dog's. Sometimes you just have to trust someone, and that's all there is to it.

experimentation:
part one
ji eun oh

Tonight is a Saturday night. Halloween night, and I am sitting at home. I am sitting at home because I am grounded, and it is all because of our stupid science experiment for which I am now writing this stupid report.

Of course, being grounded has given me plenty of opportunity to contemplate the supernatural, as I have handed out Mars bars to ghosts and devils and witches and angels. All pretend, of course.

It is easy to pretend. To pass a scientific test is not so easy. If there is one thing our research group has managed to prove, that would be it.

The first experiment our group did was a pretest to increase our chances of finding somebody with ESP. We got as many people as we could to do the Zener ESP card test. We decided to do more testing on only the subjects who scored the best. That way we'd eliminate the definitely nonpsychic duds.

The way a pretest works is, somebody shuffles the twenty-five cards and puts them in a box. Once the experimenter is ready, the subject is supposed to guess the order of the cards inside the box and write it on the answer sheet.

Marina got some people from her ESL class to take the test after school in the library. One spoke Spanish, one spoke Mandarin. One spoke Korean, and she got very excited when she saw me. But I don't remember how to say anything in Korean besides the menu at No Da Gi and the Lord's Prayer, which you can't say in school anyhow.

A girl named Kamala got a pretty good score, but it had to be luck. After all, she couldn't even understand the directions.

Then there were the people Kathleen brought in from special ed. They couldn't understand the directions, either. Kathleen tried to explain to them. I am the head experimenter, but they listened to her way better than they listened to me. One of them was a hair-sniffer, like Kathleen. I actually had to wear a bun for the rest of the week. I hope everyone appreciates my sacrifice for the sake of science.

Brandon couldn't get any of his friends (not that I've noticed him having any friends in Waverly) to come in for a dumb experiment, as he called it. He finally dragged in his little brothers. They were very cute, I have to admit, but little Michael was more interested in wiggling his front tooth than finishing the test. Hosea got a pretty good score, but you can't get useful results from just one run, and he never came back to do any more.

Ben was even less successful at recruiting subjects than Brandon. He got none.

Unlike Ben, I have tons of friends. In fact, I found seventeen people who agreed to be tested. I did most of them over the phone, since I have my own line. My parents were happy I was using it for homework for once. (I didn't tell them *which* homework.) Unfortunately, it wasn't much help. I have seventeen definitely unpsychic friends.

That doesn't count my five unpsychic Mad Science acquaintances who also took the test. Check out our so-called *Data:*

Name: *Benjamin D. Lloyd*	
Target Card	Subject's Guess
+	□
∼	+
□	★
★	∼
★	○
+	□
∼	+
□	★
□	∼
□	○
○	□
★	+
○	★
+	∼
∼	○
★	□
∼	+
+	★
□	∼
★	○
○	□
∼	+
○	★
○	∼
+	○

Total Correct: 0/25 = 0 percent

Experimenter Comments: A historic moment—Ben's worst test grade.

Subject Comments: Actually, Ji, the space above is intended for test-related observations. Examples of this would include ambient noise in the room (you talking to your friends), stomach growling (yours), etc. Also, I *have* previously scored 0 percent on a P.E. test on lay-ups. But I'm glad to know that you weren't paying attention during that class, either.

May I also point out that my test results here are noteworthy for being significantly *lower* than those expected by chance (which would be five correct, or 20 percent). Could this abysmal score be significant in the case of a non–ESP believer like me? Perhaps I just wasn't trying very hard. Though if I had wanted to skew the results, believe me, I would have guessed the same symbol twenty-five times and been assured of attaining a decent score of 20 percent.

Name: *Marina*	
Target Card	Subject's Guess
+	○
~~	+
□	★
★	~~~
★	★
+	~~~
~~	+
□	★
□	~~~
□	○
○	□
★	+
○	★
+	~~~
~~	○
★	+
~~	★
+	+
□	★
★	~~~
○	□
~~	+
○	★
○	~~~
+	○

Total Correct: 2/25 = 8 percent

Experimenter Comments: Poor English does not count as an excuse when the whole test involves symbols.

Subject Comments: I do not know why Ji should ask about my strategy for this test when I do so bad, but of course I will tell. For each question, when I try to make the right answer I think of a person in our Mad Science class. Who comes into my mind first, I pick and match them to their symbol. Ben, he is like the square,[1] straight and even on each side. Kat, she is the circle, arms always open to embrace. The lines are Claire with the curly hair that is filled with static. The plus sign is like the gold necklace Ji wears when I first see her, and that she often moves to touch now since it is gone. And Brandon—he is the basketball star.

Why have I not included myself in this list? Ji wants to know. Well, I did not once think of me. Now that she asks, I realize—how could I choose which symbol to be? On the basketball court, I put my arms out and make a square that no one can penetrate. I am energy, like those lines. Positive plus energy that I must give to Babushka, as Mama and Papa remind me plenty more often than they need to. The circle forms in my mind an Olympic ring, which is the symbol I would *wish* to choose for me when I go play on the basketball team for American women. I like to think I am humble and therefore will not call myself Star. But the Star of David pendant Babushka has hidden in her denture powders must be meant for me on my thirteenth birthday. Yes?

---

[1] Actually, it's a rectangle, and thus not so equilateral as it appears. —BDL

Name: *Brandon*	
Target Card	Subject's Guess
+	O
≋	O
□	O
★	O
★	O
+	O
≋	O
□	O
□	O
□	O
O	O
★	O
O	O
+	O
≋	O
★	O
≋	O
+	O
□	O
★	O
O	O
≋	O
O	O
O	O
+	O

TOTAL CORRECT: 5/25 = 20 percent

EXPERIMENTER COMMENTS: Does this even count?

SUBJECT COMMENTS: Ji said close my eyes and pick the symbol in my heart. My grandma would think I was being lazy and not trying here, but that's not it. This is the answer I get every time. The ESP books call it circle. I call it big, fat, empty zero. But at least that's not my grade — this time.

Name: _Ji_	
Target Card	**Subject's Guess**
+	O
≋	+
□	O
★	□
★	O
+	★
≋	≋
□	O
□	★
□	★
O	≋
★	□
O	★
+	□
≋	□
★	+
≋	+
+	≋
□	+
★	O
O	≋
≋	□
O	≋
O	★
+	+

Total Correct: 2/25 = 8 percent

Experimenter Comments: Test scored by Ben Lloyd to prevent possibility of cheating. —BDL

Subject Comments: As if I care about my grade on this.

Name: *Claire*	
Target Card	Subject's Guess
+	〰
〰	〰
□	○
★	□
★	○
+	★
〰	〰
□	○
□	★
□	★
○	○
★	□
○	○
+	□
〰	〰
★	+
〰	+
+	〰
□	+
★	★
○	○
〰	□
○	○
○	○
+	+

Total Correct: 10/25 = 40 percent

Experimenter Comments: Re-test and see if above-chance score is repeatable.

Subject Comments: I wonder how I did that?

Name: *Kathleen*	
Target Card	Subject's Guess
+	+
∼	○
□	○
★	★
★	★
+	★
∼	∼
□	○
□	★
□	□
○	○
★	□
○	○
+	□
∼	+
★	+
∼	+
+	∼
□	□
★	★
○	○
∼	□
○	○
○	+
+	+

Total Correct: 12/25 = 48 percent

Experimenter Comments: Re-test. We will never hear the end of the first test where Kathleen got a higher grade than Claire.

Subject Comments: Higher than you, too, Ji Oh.

Name: *Claire, second test*	
Target Card	**Subject's Guess**
≋	□
○	≋
★	+
≋	+
○	≋
□	+
○	≋
★	○
□	★
○	★
+	○
★	□
□	○
○	□
□	≋
+	+
★	+
≋	≋
★	+
□	★
≋	○
+	□
+	○
≋	○
+	+

TOTAL CORRECT: 3/25 = 12 percent

EXPERIMENTER COMMENTS: Took twice as long as previous test. Lots of daydreaming going on.

SUBJECT COMMENTS: I had trouble concentrating. I could only think how much Kathleen was going to hate me if I did better than her the second time. Not that I believe I'm psychic or anything, but is it possible that worrying affected my score?

Name: *Kathleen, second test*	
Target Card	Subject's Guess
∿	☺
○	☺
★	☺
∿	☺
○	☺
□	☺
○	☺
★	☺
□	☺
○	☺
+	☺
★	☺
□	☺
○	☺
□	☺
+	☺
★	☺
∿	☺
★	☺
□	☺
∿	☺
+	☺
+	☺
∿	☺
+	☺

TOTAL CORRECT: N/A

EXPERIMENTER COMMENTS: Subject smart enough to quit while ahead.

SUBJECT COMMENTS: I don't want to play anymore.

It was pretty weird when Claire and Kathleen got those good results the first time. A lot of their guesses were the same, too. If I wasn't watching them every second, I'd swear somebody was cheating.

I tend to think along those lines because I'm an expert cheater. All those times Claire thought I was so good at Pictionary, she never guessed I was just looking at the card. Which is why I can't believe Claire could have extra-special powers of perception. Sometimes I don't think she even has *regular* powers of perception. I've tried so many times to clue her in — nicely — about what people are saying behind her back. About her poodle hair, and that hyena laugh, and the people (the ones who care, which is not many) who ask me why can't she just relax and have fun. Then of course there are the nonstop comments about Kathleen. Maybe Claire's just gotten used to blocking it all out.

Teachers always call on Claire, which I guess she can't help, but it's also not a great thing when you're trying to make other people like you. Of course when Mr. Ennis wanted an update on our Mad Science experiment, he asked Claire.

She told him what we had that was usable in our report, which was basically nothing. Kathleen did not like to hear that her results didn't matter, and she really did not like to hear it when Ben suggested that we had shown ESP was 99.9 percent unlikely to exist (or something like that). He'd worked up some statistics to prove it. Mr. Ennis said they didn't prove anything. But if we wanted to quit now, that was fine. We just couldn't take the project to the science fair — even the lame one at our school. Because it wasn't any good.

Mr. Ennis took a vote to see if we should keep going. The results were very surprising (at least to a nonpsychic person like me).

Kathleen raised her hand first. "We like this experiment."

"We do?" Ben asked.

"We, as in me and Kathleen," Claire clarified. This was called appeasing Kathleen.

"Ah," Marina said. "American democracy." She looked at Kathleen. "What the group wants — this is the way I vote."

"You're so good to me, Marina." Kathleen hugged her. "Ooh, you smell so good. Sausage."

Brandon saw Kathleen eyeing his flattop and used his legs to tip his chair backward. "If you're gonna sniff me, I'm voting no."

Kathleen sighed. "But you have such nice hair."

"I'm voting no anyway."

"Chair legs on the floor," Mr. Ennis said. "What's your vote, Ji?"

I had to think about it. I mean, I was pretty sure we would never find the evidence to prove our hypothesis. But I was still more curious about ESP than, say, the Hubble constant, which I could tell was the suggestion on Ben's lips. "I say we stay with our experiment," I said.

Claire looked at me and smiled. Why was she smiling? If

she really had ESP, she'd know I wanted to yell: Do we always have to vote the same way? Do the same things? Mad Science?! But I could never say that to her. So I just smiled back. Claire doesn't get the concept of the fake smile at all. At least you always know she means it when she's acting friendly. Not that that's too often lately.

Anyhow, it was decided. ESP won. And this time it wasn't because of a roll of the dice.

The dice did come in handy for our psychokinesis (P.K.) experiment, where subjects are asked to will the dice to fall a particular way.

Claire's score sheet (the only one worth looking at) will demonstrate how this test worked — or didn't work, I guess we could say.

Claire	
Desired Die Roll	Actual Die Roll
1	1
1	1
1	5
1	1
2	3
2	2
2	2
2	4
3	5
3	5
3	6
3	4
4	2
4	1
4	1
4	1
5	6
5	4
5	3
5	4
6	5
6	6
6	2
6	3

You will note that things were going along pretty well through the twos. I was thinking that suddenly I didn't feel so bad about Claire always beating me at Sorry! and Monopoly and the Game of Life. (Why do you think I decided to start cheating at Pictionary?)

But things started to go bad during the threes. That's when Mrs. Gershwin, the school librarian, came over to us. She was upset that we were using the library for gambling.

Although we were of course not gambling and Mrs. Gershwin is of course clueless (she didn't notice our dice use for two weeks), she was right when she said that our project was turning out like crap. (Actually, what she said was craps. Hello?!)

Since Marina thought this was a good thing (having recently learned about Maryland crabs in ESL class), we were then treated to an in-depth explanation of the digestive process by Ben Lloyd. It also marked the occasion of Marina's first English swear word. (Although she knew lots of Russian ones and even some Spanish ones, which she was happy to teach us in return. I wish I knew some Korean ones, but my parents don't believe in swear words.)

Anyhow, by the time this was all sorted out and we were able to restart Claire's P.K. test in Mr. Ennis's room after school, she was no longer on a roll.

We therefore remained without a shred of scientific evidence for ESP. No statistically significant results. Just a few glimmers of weirdness.

I will now save myself some work by including an article from the *Waverly Times* that explains what happened next.

The Waverly Times

October 15

Teachers Cry Foul in Basketball Defeat

Clearview Newcomer Wins Points, Friends

by Joanna Robles
Staff Writer

WITH twenty seconds remaining, sweat beaded on Marina Krenina's upper lip. Her elbow was scraped and her knees bruised. The ball burned against her fingertips. She had to get rid of it, to take one last shot at victory.

The score was 59–57. Clearview teachers were winning—poised to grab their sixth straight victory in the annual student-faculty basketball game.

The ball left Marina's hands and arced through the air. The sound of the generator pulsed like a heartbeat in the hushed auditorium.

Claire Phelps, 12, stood in her seat, eyes closed. She couldn't bring herself to watch the slow trajectory of the ball, traveling on its seemingly unmistakable path to foul territory oblivion.

Victory banners waved in the faculty section of the bleachers.

"Go in, go in, go in!" Claire shouted.

The ball appeared to pause in midair. It hung, suspended, for an agonizing moment. Then it veered to the right, dropping through the hoop as though magnetized.

The collective sigh of the audience mingled with the swish of the net. A spell of silence was woven, only to be broken moments later by the sound of the buzzer, jolting the crowd into applause.

Team member Brandon Kelly, 13, laughed as Marina shook his outstretched palm. She seemed puzzled when he gave her a hearty slap in return.

An immigrant from Moscow two months ago, Marina may be unfamiliar with slapping five or other social conventions of American basketball. But on the court, she couldn't be more at home.

"My whole family, they are gymnasts," she explained. "My father and my mother, coaches. I do not wish to be the different one. But I am so tall." Marina pulled herself up to her full five feet, demonstrating how she towered over her 4'8" grandmother.

"My grandmother, she gives me basketball when I am little girl. This way, she says, I can do sports, too. She is my first coach. When her heart is healthy, we play every day." Marina smiled. "She whip my butt every day."

"I am happy when she plays," said Irina Markova, 62, through an interpreter. "But I do not like the way they do here. So rough. I want them to treat my granddaughter nice."

Borne out of the gymnasium on the shoulders of her fellow team members, Marina said she had no complaints about the way she's been treated in Waverly. And she attributed her game-winning heroics not to a hard-won hook shot, but to the good wishes of newfound friend Claire Phelps. "She said to the ball to go in the net, and it did," Marina said. She squeezed her grandmother's hand. "It is good here. People are very kind. My grandmother will see."

A few days after the basketball game, we had a school holiday — Yom Kippur, I think. A whole bunch of us were going to go to a sidewalk sale at the mall in the afternoon. Claire loves the mall but she hates my new friends, so I was surprised when she decided to come. I prayed that Kathleen would not invite herself along and ruin the day for all of us. And, of course, that Claire would not get all moody and ruin the day just for me.

Shockingly enough, Ben announced in Mad Science the week before that he didn't have any plans for the holiday. Therefore, he proposed that we use part of our day off to work on our experiment.

Marina called him loco. (She learned that in ESL class, mistakenly thinking it was an English word.) Brandon applauded her for making everyone laugh. Everyone but Ben.

"What if I pay you to come to my house and work on our project?" Ben asked us.

That sure got our attention.

Eighty-three dollars and thirty-three cents apiece, Ben said. More per person if not everyone showed. Leave it to Ben to come up with a ridiculous amount like $83.33. But when I asked him about it, he only shrugged.

"You think you can bribe us?" Brandon asked Ben.

"Yep."

I looked at Claire. He could certainly bribe us — after all, we could make a mall trip anytime. "Where are you going to get that much money?" I asked Ben.

"You'll find out on Wednesday morning," he said. And that was all he would tell us.

Claire and I thought we'd go straight from Ben's to the mall. But we never did make it there. By the time I got the money, I wound up donating it to the food bank. I couldn't imagine myself ever wearing a sweater that would only remind me of everything that happened. But more on that later.

Since I knew I would be responsible for the Experiment section of the report, I put my journalism skills to good use and took extremely neat and detailed notes on the meeting, as follows: (Please excuse my day planner — I ran out of paper.)

Date: Wednesday, October 14
Time: 9:23 a.m.
Place: 10632 Thunderclap Drive, Ben Lloyd's house
Weather: Raining again!
Arrived with Claire and Kathleen, late, as usual
Ben and Brandon already there

Ben asks us for money—50¢ each. Makes no
mention of paying us anything, but predicts we
will be winners. Tells us Marina is off saying
prayers for us in temple, but apparently she paid
in advance.

Me: Prayers? Don't you want to depend on science
to win the science fair?

Ben: With a topic like ours? I'll take any help we
can get.

Kathleen: Do you really think we're gonna win the
science fair, Ben?

Ben: I was referring to the lottery. But yes, I really think we're going to win the science fair.

Brandon: (laughter) The lottery? That's how we're gonna get our big bucks?

Ben: That's right.

Brandon: Aw, man.

Claire: (hyena laugh) There goes our mall money.

Me: (silent swearing as I check my watch)

Ben takes out a notebook filled with numbers. Claims he's used a spreadsheet program to do some kind of statistical thing on numbers that won the Pick 3 game in Maryland. Based on "the laws of probability and the tendency of the distribution to become uniform as it approaches infinity" (whatever the hell that means), he's picked the number 305 to win sometime soon.

Brandon: If people could really do that, the lottery would go broke.

Ben: If there really was ESP, the lottery would go broke.

Kathleen: Is that true, Ben?

Ben: I propose that we find out.

Kathleen: (sniffing Ben's breath) Did you have pepperoni pizza for breakfast, Ben?

Brandon: (throws pizza box in air) She's psychic! I'm telling you, Lloyd. We can all go home right now.

Unfortunately, no one breaks for the door.

Ben says that every day for four weeks we'll play his number as well as a number chosen by "psychic" means. In the (very unlikely) event that we win today, he wants only a "bargain initiation fee" of 50¢ from each of us.

Ben: Possibly, we will be rich. Possibly, we will have an indication as to whether ESP can triumph over science.

Claire: Possibly we will be poor and have no answers, either.

Ben: Possibly.

Brandon: What if we say no?

Ben: You don't get the money.

Claire: What if we say yes and we don't win? You promised if we came to your house today and did what you said, we'd get—

Ben: That's right. And what I say is, if everyone gives me 50¢ and somebody gives me a winning lottery number, the money is yours. Ours.

Brandon: (instantly) No fair.

Me: Fair or not, I'm in.

I mean, how often do you get to gamble for homework? My parents (majorly) disapprove of gambling, but they (obviously) approve of homework. Maybe not the supernatural kind, but no way do I plan to mention that part.

Claire tries to put in 50¢ for Kathleen, who of course throws a huge tantrum and says she wants to win with her own money. (Usually being nice to Kathleen does not exactly pay.)

Ben: (cheerful now with money in hand) Okay. Let's talk logistics.

Brandon: Let's talk English, if you don't mind.

Me: How's this for logistics? Where are we going to get a psychic?

Ben looks at Claire.

Claire: Not me!

Ben: Besides your early dice success and the amazing hooking basketball, you scored above chance on the Zener card test. That makes you our best bet.

Kathleen: (trembly voice) I got a good score, too. (more trembly) I did good, too!!

Claire: (grimacing, eyes closed, fists clenched) No!!!!

A moment passes. Silence hangs in the air like Marina's big hook shot while we wait for Kathleen to erupt.

She does not. Not a sniffle, not a tear, not a pout.

It's almost enough to make me believe in P.K. But obviously if Claire had powers like that, she would have used them a long time ago.

Claire makes Ben let her and Kathleen pick a number together. This does not seem very scientific to me, but I guess Ben doesn't care. He's so sure his 305 number is going to win.

Claire and Kathleen huddle. Somehow—don't ask me how—they agree on a number. 715.

Ben writes on a little piece of paper: #715, then #305. Next he writes: 2 Pick Three Maryland Lottery Tickets. $2. Butter pecan ice cream.

Coupon. He slides two dollars and the coupon under the paper and says his dad will buy the tickets.

By 10:30, we are on our way out the door. Since Kathleen did not bring any money (was counting on the $83.33) and throws a tantrum, we do not get to go to the mall. Plus I have no ride home, so I will be stuck at the Phelps house till 6 p.m., when my mom can finally pick me up. Oh, yay.

OCTOBER

Sunday	school paper Monday deadline	social studies quiz Tuesday	Mad Science Wednesday	Mr. Mathews Thursday after school	Friday	Saturday
				1	2 Editorial Mtg. – 3:30 (bring artwork)	3
4	5 piano – 4:30 call Brian re church choir – 7	6 student council – 3:30 Baby-sit Meghann 5-7	7 ESP Testing 10-11 2:30-4	8 Start Reading Waverly Times ESP Testing 2:30-3	9 cover student-faculty b-ball game 2 p.m.	10
11 Algebra @ Claire's	12 Algebra Test piano – 4:00 ESP Testing – 6-8	13 🎵 AUDITIONS Meghann 5-7	14 9—Ben's house NO SCHOOL 2:00 Macy's!!	15 B-Day Day Katie Claire/Kat →	16 mall 6:00 buy Halloween costume Katie—purple skirt Kathleen—stuffed dog Claire—??	17 Katie's B-Day Party Claire/ Kathleen
18	19 piano – 4:30 church choir – 7	20 student council – 3:30 BRING SODAS! No Meghann	21	22 cover soccer game Feature interview w/Brian ☺	23 🎵 Dance	24 volunteer at soup kitchen – 10
25 Daylight-Saving Time Ends GROUNDED study Algebra!!	26	27 BIG LOTTERY WIN Meghann 5-7	28 Bye-Bye Mad Science!	29	30	31 Halloween Katie's Halloween party during shoot for toga!

89

Ben's dad bought our lottery tickets that same night. I watched the drawing while I was talking on the phone to Katie. The winning number was 362.

"We got one digit correct," Ben noted the next day. Then he took more of our money. Two dollars apiece to play two numbers a day for six days.

Altogether, we wasted a total of $15 that first week with a return of $0.

"I can't pay my two dollars this week," Kathleen said the next time Ben asked for cash. "I'm saving my money to buy a ticket for the Halloween dance."

"I'll pay your two dollars this week," Claire offered.

Kathleen crossed her arms. "No."

"You can pay me back."

"No," Kathleen said again.

"You know what?" I said. "I'm with Kathleen. I don't want to pay, either. It's a waste. We're never going to win the lottery."

"Okay, wait. Let me see if I got this straight," Brandon said. "It comes down to some dumb dance or five hundred big ones, and you pick the dance? Think about it. Your future, Ji. Come on."

"I am," I said. "Claire and Kathleen are not psychic, we are not going to win the lottery, and I don't want to waste any more money." Anyhow, who was to say my future wasn't with Brian Murtaugh? The dance could be very important to my future.

"One more week," Ben said. "One more week, and if we

don't win, we'll quit." He turned to Kathleen. "And I'll buy you a ticket to the dance. Okay?"

"You mean like a date? You'll be my date to the dance, Ben?"

"Um . . ." Ben blinked. Claire got out the tissues and gave Ben a look. "I . . . Yeah, I'll be your date, Kathleen," Ben finally said. Kathleen threw her arms around him. "I guess that means I have to go, huh?" Ben gave a nervous laugh.

Mom and Dad both had to work late the night of the dance, so they made me get a ride with Claire's mom.

"This seems to be turning into a Mad Science field trip," Ben observed from the front seat.

I hung my head, and the point of my witch's hat accidentally poked between his shoulder blades.

"Ouch," Ben said.

My sentiments exactly.

School was decorated with scarecrows and cobwebs and scowling pumpkins. The lights were flickery and dim (thank God). Princess Claire and Kathleen the cat and Ben the astronaut (complete with authentic *moon rocks* from his astronomer father) and I almost managed to slip in unnoticed.

Then Kathleen let out a bloodcurdling scream.

"Blood!" she shrieked.

Two hundred people turned to stare at us.

But Kathleen was right. There was a trail of blood on the gold carpet outside the gym. And — much more gross — a tail. A lizard's tail.

"Gosh," Claire said. "What . . . interesting decorations."

Marina and Brandon (dressed with stunning originality as basketball players — complete with sweat) came over to us and peered at the tail.

"Not decoration," Marina said. "When I am on Junior Olympic basketball team for Russia, we travel to Guam, and my grandmother accompany me. I practice and practice, and for two minutes I play in one game. Two minutes. Babushka chase gecko lizards with a broom in the night. The most exciting part of the trip. This tail . . ." — she pointed at the tail, which began to flop around on its own — "real."

I had the weirdest creepy-crawly sensation all of a sudden. Like something slithering over my feet. I shivered.

"Oh, no," Kathleen moaned. "Mr. Ennis's lizard can't be dead. Not like Alice. Not Lily the lizard, too."

"Do not worry, Kathleen. Lizards lose their tails when they are frightened and run away," Marina said. "Probably Lily is fine."

"Really?" Kathleen said. "But—" She grabbed Claire's arm. "Doesn't it hurt to lose a part of you?"

"Sure does," Brandon said softly.

Marina looked up at him. "I know, Brandon. I know." She paused. "But if small change lets you live, you can do it gladly." She sighed. "This I am telling Babushka all the time."

As usual, I didn't have any idea what Marina was talking about, but the conversation was definitely headed in an even more un-fun direction. I decided this was a good time to make my exit. "Well, there's Katie and Brian," I said as I hitched up my skirt. "I'm going to go say hi."

"Wait," Claire said. "I'll come, too."

I almost screamed. Did she have to be so clingy all the time? Did she learn that from Kathleen? Did she even know how much they were alike that way?

"Us, too." Kathleen pulled Ben behind her. The moon rocks swung around and hit me in the butt. I heard somebody start laughing. I saw somebody pointing.

Under the green makeup, I felt my face turn red. I couldn't stand it. I couldn't stand being with these people for one more minute. I wasn't Kathleen's twin. *We* weren't attached at the hip. I mean, she didn't even *like* me.

I told Claire she could come. But please, not Kathleen and Ben and the moon rocks.

Usually Claire would have said fine. No big deal.

But this time — don't ask me why — she turned white between her freckles. "No," she whispered. And then she said it again, cold and sharp. "No."

I felt much smaller than my actual height, which is 4'8". I felt as though I were nothing — air — and Claire could see right through me.

Claire took a deep breath. "Come on, Kathleen. Let's get away from this witch we used to call Ji."

"Witch with a B," Kathleen said, and she followed Claire and Ben to the food table.

If I had been using my brain, I would never have gone after them.

"Um, um . . . why don't we dance?" Ben asked Claire.

I thought of Ben flapping his elbows at the fourth-grade square dance. Claire had traded partners with me so I didn't have to get stepped on by him.

Claire has never really minded getting stepped on, but still I didn't expect her to take Ben's hand and say, "Yes."

This was definitely the spookiest Halloween of my life.

"Witches use lizards' tails, you know," Kathleen said to me, "in their potions and stuff."

I took off my witch's hat. "Cats eat lizards."

Kathleen's cat whiskers began to tremble, and Claire dropped Ben's hand.

"I didn't kill Lily!" Kathleen cried. "I didn't do it, I didn't do it!"

If I'd wanted to prevent the whole seventh grade from staring at me, it was definitely too late now. I looked for Brian, but there were so many people behind so many masks that I couldn't recognize anybody's face. Why hadn't I worn a mask?

"We have to find Lily," Kathleen sobbed. "We have to find her and help her before something bad happens. You try, Claire." She gulped. "Use your ESP."

"Gosh," Claire said. "Uh . . ."

"The psychic detectives I read about," Ben volunteered, rolling his eyes at Claire, "when they look for a missing person, they usually try holding an object that belonged to that person and see if they can get some . . . you know, vibes or something."

"But all we have of Lily," Claire said, "is her—"

"Tail," Ben finished.

"That is quite all right," Marina said cheerfully. "It is no problem to touch."

Marina reached down and pinched it between her fingers. "See? Here."

I could not believe Kathleen had just asked for Claire's help. And even more, I could not believe Claire was going to hold a lizard's tail in her sweaty little hand and pretend that there was anything she could do for Kathleen or for Lily at this point.

Claire took a deep breath as she watched the tail twitch its way from Marina's hands into hers. She closed her eyes.

"Claire—" Kathleen said.

"Shh," Claire replied, her eyes squeezed shut. "I'm concentrating."

Her face was translucent white. Dots from the strobe lights flickered across her eyelids.

"I'm getting a word," she said at last.

"A word?" Marina asked.

"Go."

Kathleen's whiskers twitched hopefully. "Go?"

"That's it," Claire said finally. "I have a sense of evil. Foreboding. Go. That's the word. I don't know."

And she looked right at me. The haunted house music creaked and groaned in a minor key. E minor. I thought about what go meant. When your name is Ji Oh, you don't forget what it spells. Of course I didn't do anything to Lily the lizard. I thought about why Claire would say it with her face glowing green in the light that night. The thought I had at that moment (though I should probably not include it in a formal report) was *Go to hell, Claire Phelps.*

I called my parents to come pick me up from the dance. I didn't know what else to do. I couldn't stay there. I just couldn't. I didn't even get one dance with Brian. Two more months till I have another chance.

Mom sat on my bed that night and tried to talk to me about what happened. I didn't feel like talking.

"Ji Eun," she said, "life is changing. You are growing up. You must make your own way, your own happiness."

That's when she spotted the Zener cards. They were buried under like thirteen things, but Mom has sharp eyes.

She slid one out with her fingertip, as though she didn't dare touch it. "Now I see why you have been unhappy," she said. "You look for truth in all the wrong places."

Then she went and got Dad. And I got the Lecture.

Mom had heard about the lizard tail from one of her church friends who was chaperoning the dance. The *Halloween* dance. She must have been thinking Satan worship when she was untying my witch's cape and stroking my chin. "We worry for you, Ji Eun. Why you don't come to church with us. Why you have so many new friends at school."

My parents explained that they did not feel I should be dabbling in the supernatural. The supernatural was incompatible with their religion.

They did not understand why I found this funny. And I did not understand why I should be grounded for *doing my homework*.

What I wanted to say was, if there was no such thing as the supernatural, I didn't see how there could be such a thing as God. But of course I couldn't say that. Not to my parents. Not out loud. Not at all.

For the first time in a long time, I needed something from Claire. Even if she was mad at me . . . she'd understand my unreasonable family. Even after everything that had just happened. Nobody knew more about unreasonable relatives than Claire.

I punched the autodial button, number 1, not even labeled.

"I'm on the other line with Ben," she said the instant she heard my voice. She sounded so unfriendly that for a second, I thought she was Kathleen. "I can't talk now."

Ben, the most unpopular person in the seventh grade, was more important to her than me. Me.

I hung up the phone. My hand was shaking when it erased her number from autodial.

We never did talk. We haven't talked. I don't think we will talk.

As I promised my parents, I left the Mad Science Club on Wednesday morning. That's when Ben informed me that we had won the lottery the night before. He counted out my money silently. He refused to tell me whether the winning number was Claire's or his, since I was no longer a member of the experimental team and could not be trusted with their secrets. I don't know why, but I couldn't help looking up the numbers later in the *Waverly Times*. I should have known Ben's didn't win. Why else wouldn't he tell me?

Anyhow, this is where my participation in the experiment ended. Therefore, the remainder of this Experimentation section will be completed by Claire Phelps. I look forward to reading it at the school science fair and seeing how the project turned out. And what lovely things Claire has to say about me.

paranormal pursuits: dreams
brandon kelly

I DIDN'T USE TO REMEMBER MY DREAMS. HARDLY ever. Now I wake up with them sometimes, and I don't even know what bed I'm in. I sit up and think I'm about to whack my head on the basketball hoop. But of course it's not there. This isn't even my own bed, but Ma's from when she was a kid.

I slept here, too, a long time ago, sometimes when I would have nightmares and Ma would let me come in with her. I can still remember that, but I never remembered my bad dreams in those days, not even the next morning.

Maybe the bed brings back the dreams—I don't know. Maybe it's this project even. Ben's ESP books say your dreams can predict the future sometimes. They say to keep journals of your dreams and see if they come true.

I don't need any journal. I have one dream. It goes like this.

We are in Kim's grocery and the bullet comes through

the window. It hits Ma, and she falls down — right there in front of me. Even though she taught me CPR, I stand there and don't know what to do. Her blood is running and running over my hands until it's clear, like pickle juice. Because it all came out of her already. And she's dead.

I guess that's the only part of my future I can picture. Ma still being dead.

Last night I heard Grandma snoring in her bedroom so loud I couldn't fall asleep. I remembered how we were in this room, Ma and me, when I was real little. And she was singing this song to me. Ma was tone-deaf, so I got rap lullabies. And there was Grandma in the other room, snoring out the beat.

How come to hear Grandma's big old nose used to make me feel so warm and safe? Now it just grates on me until I want to yell. Because I want to sleep so bad. I want to sleep and sleep and not have to wake up again. Not in this bed in Waverly. Not to one more day without Ma.

I wonder if Michael sleeps as good as he always did. And Hosea. What kind of dreams does he have? But I'm afraid to ask him, because I think maybe I don't want to know. And Grandma. When she cries at nighttime. Is she seeing Ma dead, too?

experimentation:
part two
claire phelps

AT FIRST NOBODY KNEW THAT WE'D WON THE LOT-
tery. Then there was a day when everyone knew. I'm not
sure what happened, but my hypothesis is that Ji told a
popular person.

As much as I've been thinking about popularity, I never
would have guessed it could be caused by a science project.
But all of a sudden, *everybody* wanted to talk to the Mad Scientists. Even eighth-graders. It made me so nervous that I
told Ben we couldn't play anymore. I couldn't take the pres-
sure. $83.33 was enough for me. Besides, after Ji and I
stopped speaking I lost my urge to shop. I gave my money
to Kathleen, who bought a karaoke machine. I was obviously
not using precognition, since I haven't had a peaceful
night's sleep since.

This is how everybody else spent the money:

Marina: Fresh vegetables (for Babushka) and Snickers (for
herself)

Ben: College fund

Brandon: High-tops — size six, ladies'

Ji: I can pretty safely guess clothes or shoes

I assume that Ji has already described my experiences with the lottery, as well as the Zener cards, the dice, the basketball game. I also assume I know what she said about them. The same thing I thought. Luck. That's all. Not ESP. Definitely not.

By the time we got to our winter choir concert, our experiment was basically over. I had been working on the telepathy thing for over a month. Kathleen didn't even seem to know that I was trying. Mom did remark once or twice on the unusual "holiday cheer" in our household. Well, it must have been pretty glum last year, because I didn't see that I was making any progress at all in understanding my sister.

But at that concert — for the first time — I started thinking there really might be something to our hypothesis. That there might be ESP.

It's true that when I took the Zener card test, I imagined myself making those cards — drawing a box or drawing a circle. So that when I drew the box or the circle on my answer sheet, it didn't feel like guessing. Not exactly.

It's also true that, when I knew Kathleen wanted me to fail, I failed. Did she make that happen? Did I?

I didn't really think so. It wasn't like I could suddenly see into the future, or — even better — change it. I couldn't do something big, like make Kathleen normal. Or make *me* normal. I couldn't even do something small, like make her smile.

I could just sit in the audience at the choir concert like always. Smile and clap. Hope she would stand quietly in her place and not make a scene.

Every time there's a choir concert, Kathleen prays she will get a solo. Every time, it goes to Ji. To make up for this, Kathleen sings loudly enough to be heard over the other eighty people.

Ji has a pretty voice. It's clear and high. When she sings, I can feel my heart beat faster. The same thing happens to me when Kathleen sings, but that's just nerves.

"Said the night wind to the little lamb, 'Do you see what I see?'" Ji sang. "'Do you hear what I hear?'"

Kathleen's favorite song. Do you hear what I hear? Because she knows other people don't see and hear and know the same way she does. Sometimes I think she's so incredibly smart. And other times . . . you just wonder where she's getting these ideas in her head.

But I'll say this — Kathleen knew about Ji. She always knew. Ji needed to be in the middle of things, and so did Kathleen. Only one person can be in the middle. And in my life, it will always be Kathleen.

My heart felt like a lump of clay when I listened to Ji sing. From one song to the next, it was just words. Words about raising up the humble, the lowly, the baby who slept among the animals and loved them and sang with them.

The music flowed out of her, smooth and beautiful and pure; then, in my ears, it curdled.

At first I thought I was dreaming. The piano hiccupped, and even though Mrs. Keepers, the choir teacher, was pressing keys, no sound was coming out. Mrs. Keepers flung her hands into the air. Her feet inched backward, away from the choir and the music and the piano like they were possessed.

Someone tapped my shoulder, and I jumped out of my seat.

"Did you do that?" Brandon asked me. "You using those P.K. powers of yours?"

Of course I didn't do that. I wouldn't *ruin* Ji's choir solo. How could I do that? How do you make a piano stop playing?

"Uh-oh," Brandon said. "What's your sister doing now?"

Kathleen was climbing down from her choir riser in the second row. She ran to the piano and threw open the lid. Then she stuck her hands in without looking and came out with a snake. A wrung-out-looking snake with a little bulge in the middle. Alice.

Kathleen kissed the snake.

The choir risers emptied. The audience buzzed. Someone turned up the lights just as Kathleen laid Alice in Mr. Ennis's arms.

"How did you know?" I heard him ask. He was sitting with Brandon, behind me. "How did you know it was Alice?"

"She told me," Kathleen whispered.

As crazy as it sounds, I believed Kathleen really might have heard it from the snake's forked tongue.

"Go was the clue. You said Go would help us find Lily the lizard," Kathleen told me. "You were right. We found her during Ji Oh's solo. Ji Oh – G-O – Go. Only . . ." — Kathleen frowned — "only you didn't say Lily would be dead."

"You mean the snake ate Lily?"

Kathleen bit her lip. "She couldn't help it. She was hungry."

Brandon peered at Alice. "She looks kind of different, doesn't she?" he asked Kathleen. "You're sure that's Alice and not some impostor snake?"

"Uh-huh. She just shed her skin is all. But she's the same on the inside."

"Maybe a little tougher after all she's been through," Mr. Ennis said.

Brandon reached out and tickled Alice's nose.

"She likes that," Kathleen said. She sneaked a peek at the choir. Mrs. Keepers was finally sinking back onto the piano bench, though keeping a very safe distance from the piano.

"I'd better go. They can't have the concert without me." Kathleen marched back to her spot as somebody dimmed the lights to make everyone quiet.

Kathleen climbed back onto her riser, and the crowd clapped for her. She got a standing ovation. In the middle of Ji's solo, my sister got an ovation.

My heart was pounding. Not out of nervousness. Not like anything I ever felt before.

Kathleen bowed. She thumped her chest, and the sound of my heart pulsed in my ears, louder and faster than the applause. Her thumping was the rhythm I felt inside me. Exactly the same.

Then it was over. My vital signs returned to normal.

Maybe there's no such thing, I remember thinking, as normal.

Maybe there is such a thing as ESP.

For a month we were making logos in art—our own personal logos. They were supposed to represent our hopes and dreams for the future. Ji's, for example, was a microphone head with short little pencil legs that were GOing somewhere. Mine was an eclair with a candle in it, because we started making them on my birthday.

My logo was an anonymous one. Nobody could figure out who the smoking cream puff was. Not even Kathleen. "You see," she said, "there's only one candle."

Kathleen's logo was a cat. It had orange cat fur. It was sleeping on a dog with orange dog fur.

At first I thought the dog was Sunshine. Sunshine hates cats, but she loves Kathleen.

Then, when I looked closely, I saw that the dog had freckles—like me.

Kathleen's dream for the future. How could I not have known?

I called her Kat when we were little, when I was first learning to talk. When I talked for her, because she couldn't.

I knew then what she wanted—always. How could I not know now?

A while ago when I was mad at Ji for coming late to my birthday party, she accused me of being "dependent" and "clingy." She said I must understand why this was an unattractive quality, since I spent my whole life putting up with it from Kathleen. I thought Ji must know nothing about me or Kathleen. My sister did not cling to me; she hated me.

But maybe Ji was right.

The logos reminded me of an experiment in Ben's ESP book. One person draws a picture in his mind; another person draws it on paper. Kind of like Pictionary—that game Ji and I never let my sister play with us.

Ben and I were talking on the phone one night when he asked if Kathleen and I wanted to try the drawing by telepathy experiment for real. At first I said no. I was scared to try. I was scared to show Kathleen what a clueless sister she had.

Ben said you had to take risks sometimes for the sake of science.

I hated to admit it to Ben, of all people, but I didn't really care about science.

I cared about Kathleen, Ben said. He was scared to pick up the phone and call his mom, and look where that got him. She was interested in his life only if she had to write an article about it. Ben said his mother didn't give a damn about science or respect it one iota.

What he was really saying was that his mother didn't give a damn about him or respect him one iota.

I'd talked to Ben's mother once. She interviewed me at the student-faculty basketball game. Afterward, Ji was talking to her about writing for the newspaper and even mentioned reading the *Waverly Times* for her Paranormal Pursuit. That's when Mrs. Robles told us a secret. Ji was distracted by Brian Murtaugh doing something dumb, but I heard what she said. She said she was the astrologer for the *Waverly Times*. Nobody was supposed to know, she told me, but it was a great job—interesting and fun. She said she hoped I liked my job as much when I grew up.

So Ben thought his mom wasn't interested in science. I knew Ben didn't think our project was much in the way of science. But his mother, the astrologer/reporter, would. I was sure she would.

I also knew Ben wanted to keep our project secret. But if I could risk my sanity and do this telepathy thing with Kathleen, couldn't he take a risk, too? Couldn't he reach outside himself just once? Just a little bit?

Therefore, the day after my conversation with Ben I placed a call to Joanna Robles in the newsroom at the *Waverly Times*. She remembered who I was from our basketball interview. She listened politely. My assessment of her niceness was totally correct. She agreed to come talk to us about our project. She agreed happily.

"What are you doing here?" is the way Ben greeted his

mother when he found her in Mr. Ennis's classroom on the day of the big telepathy experiment.

"That's no way to talk to your mother," Brandon said.

I thought for a minute he was kidding. He wasn't.

Joanna Robles smiled at Ben. She explained that I'd invited her to join us. I'd even given her some background information to read, so she would know what was going on. The parts of our report that were written so far—all but mine and Ji's and Brandon's—including the Paranormal Pursuits.

She said she liked the Paranormal Pursuits. They offered a lot of useful information and insight. She thought maybe they should even be included in the final report. To give it a little personality, a little pizzazz.

Ben said science did not need pizzazz. The rest of us voted to listen to the professional journalist.

Joanna Robles picked up her notepad and pencil. I noticed that she could write without looking down. That was helpful, because no matter who was talking or what was happening, she was watching Ben. Ben in charge.

Ben had Kathleen borrow a kids' dictionary from her special ed class. It was full of easy words with pictures. Then Kathleen and the dictionary got locked in the library.

I wasn't there for this part because I had to be isolated in Mr. Ennis's room. But I'm told this is how it happened.

Ben instructed Kathleen to close her eyes and open to a random page. He told her to point to a random entry, then think about that word and nothing but that word.

Next, Ben went to the supply closet and took out one piece of drawing paper, which he brought to me in Mr. Ennis's room. Mr. Ennis made sure we did not speak or communicate with each other in any way.

I sat in the room by myself for a long time — minutes, probably — and tried to tell myself this was not stupid. I could do this. I was thinking about everything. Joanna Robles and her newspaper article and Ji and Ben and Mr. Ennis and my Spanish homework. I was thinking about everything and nothing at the same time. Of course nothing happened. Nothing.

I put my pencil point on the paper, like maybe the word would draw itself. Then I looked at the empty lizard cage. That's how my brain felt, I thought. Empty.

I caught a glimpse of my reflection in the glass. My face, so different from Kathleen's.

Looking at your twin was supposed to be like looking in a mirror. Like looking inside yourself.

Kathleen could be so distracting on the outside, it was hard to see past that. Hard to look into her, and even harder to go past that — into me.

I was squeezing the pencil so hard that my fingers felt numb. I looked down.

The page lost its blankness. The picture appeared right before my eyes. Not all at once. It came in pieces — the edges first, and then the middle. Then it came in a flash of brightness that hurt my eyes. It came so clear, it startled me.

It was a sailboat, with a white sail. I couldn't read the

name on the boat, but it had six letters. The bay was the Chesapeake. The passenger was waving at someone on shore.

The pencil moved so fast. The drawing was so much faster than the thinking part.

When I was finished, I took my drawing to the library to see how I'd done. I did okay. Kathleen's word was *boat*.

Joanna Robles dropped her pencil.

But Kathleen didn't seem surprised. Not even a little bit.

"When can we try again?" was all she said.

"I'm free tomorrow," Joanna suggested. Her newspaper deadline was soon, I guess.

Joanna came back the next day, and we tried again.

It happened a little faster this time. Faster and surer and plainer. My fingertips felt warm and tingly as they drew out the picture of a big-footed golden retriever with a ball in her mouth.

But Kathleen's word was not *dog* or *ball* or even *big*. It was *Sunshine*.

When she saw the drawing fluttering in my fingers, Kathleen threw her arms around me and purred deep in her throat. "You smell all sunshiny and lemony and golden," she said. "Like a golden retriever."

"That's a compliment," I heard Ben whisper to Joanna Robles.

That's when Ji walked into the room.

Kathleen let go of my hair.

When I saw Ji's face, my words came out before I remembered we weren't speaking. "What's wrong?"

"I was looking for Marina," Ji whispered. It was Thursday afternoon. Thursday afternoon, when Ji worked in the principal's office.

Then Brandon's grandmother appeared in the doorway. She tried to take Marina outside, but Marina was already crying. Before Mrs. Mathews could say a word. Before she could tell her that her grandmother — Babushka — had had a heart attack and died that afternoon. At the hospital, she said. A peaceful death.

Brandon kicked the desk. His eyes darted around until they found the door.

But before he could move, Marina grabbed his hand. She put her head against his chest and sobbed into his sweatshirt.

A moment went by. Nobody moved.

Then Kathleen leaped up. She grabbed my purse, and the sound of the zipper ripped through the silence.

I realized I was crying, too. Not for me, but for Brandon and Marina and Ben, whose mom was right there but still as far away from him as the moon.

Kathleen pressed a tissue into my hand. I looked into her eyes and saw my own staring back at me. They were green and sparkling with tears.

Mrs. Gershwin tiptoed over to us with a big box of tissues. Brandon took one and blew. Mrs. Gershwin flinched at the noise that filled her library.

Brandon squeezed Mrs. Mathews's hand. *I am lucky*, I could almost feel him thinking. *I am lucky to have a grandma like you.*

Ji didn't cry. She never was a crier. She ran out of the library without saying anything to anyone. She always was a runner.

Then Ben went. Ben's mom right after him.

Pretty soon it was just me and Kathleen. Kathleen and me. We did not say a word. We didn't need to.

paranormal pursuits:
life after death
marina krehina

WHEN I FIRST COME TO AMERICA IT IS SUMMER-time. In front of our apartment there are pink roses and tall oak trees, and my sisters and brother turn cartwheels on the wide ribbon of sidewalk.

Our sponsor gives us a party right away to say welcome to this happy place. We gather together and tell stories and learn about the Jewish faith. At home we practice right away for our first Passover party in springtime. I drink the blackberry wine, so warm and sweet, and when it is finished I notice the glass next to mine which yet remains filled. When all eyes are closed for the hiding of the matzah, I take a small swallow. Just very small.

After the meal Mama says see how the wine is less in the glass. She has been reading about the faith and says this is because the prophet, Elijah — dead more than 2,000 years — has joined us at table and tasted the wine we have left for him, just as he does for every Seder supper in every year.

Babushka, she does not believe this has happened, especially when it is not even Passover. The wine is the same, not touched, she says. And my elder sister Yelena, she says when we have Passover for real she will measure the liquid in the glass. Yelena reminds me of Ben just a little bit.

I say this will do nothing. If you have not belief it can happen, you cannot see when it is before your eyes.

Of course I cannot now tell that I am the one to taste Elijah's wine. But I know I have not done this in old years. *Is it possible that Elijah shares with me this glass tonight?* I ask myself. Because I do not really think I drink so much as these missing milliliters.

It is like when Mr. Ennis changes the water to wine. He makes a trick with those chemicals. But I hear about this Jesus who changes water to wine long ago before chemicals are invented. This cannot then be a trick.

G is the one who tells me in Mad Science this particular story about Jesus. She says she does not know if she can believe it is true, when how can it be proved? Just as how can you prove God created the world in seven days? How can you prove there is God? How can you prove there is heaven? And if there is heaven, will Jewish people not go there?

Do Jewish people believe in heaven? she asks me then.

I say to her, Jewish people say we will see. We will open our hearts to the idea.

Babushka cannot understand these new ideas since we come to America — nice grocery stores with so much fresh fruit and vegetables; these lost Jewish customs that she never hears about until now when she is old. She says there is hard life and there is hard work and that is all. But I know one thing. If there is heaven, my Babushka will be the first to make her home there. I hope she will like it better than America.

And I, who have touched my lips where Elijah touched his, do believe there is heaven.

conclusion

marina krenina

MR. ENNIS TELLS US HE WILL BUY PIZZA IF WE WIN this science fair.

Babushka says many times that pizza is the only good thing in all of America. This always followed by: "I go back to Russia now."

There is at least one good thing in America more than pizza, I like to believe, and that is me.

When I cannot bear to hear one more time that Babushka still wants to go back, finally I throw harsh words back at her. "You want to leave me? Then go!"

The next day, she goes.

To heaven, G tells me.

Perhaps. But if it is not like Russia, Babushka will not find happiness there, either.

Kathleen and Claire tell me they make prayers for my family in their Catholic church. So, too, pray those nice people at temple. Those same people who say pepperoni is bad to eat. I tell them that is not why Babushka died —

because she ate the wrong thing. They say oh, no, of course not. Please do not believe that.

I wish I could believe that. They do not know I am thinking a much worse reason for her to leave me.

Brandon says do not blame myself that Babushka has gone. I yell at him to go away from me. He is not like Babushka. He stays.

I whisper my prayers in the quiet of the night as I touch the Star of David, so warm against my chest. *God*, I ask, *do you hear me? Babushka, do you hear me?*

No one answers me.

When Mrs. Parrot says in P.E. class that we cannot have jewelry, I will not play if I must let go this necklace.

Brandon is mad at me because our team loses. "Your grandma would not like the way you're acting," he says to me.

"You do not know my babushka," I tell him. "You never talk to her once."

He shows me the definition of ESP: The process of accumulating knowledge that cannot be gained by the use of our five known senses.

"I know you," he says. "That's enough."

"How? How is that enough?"

Brandon shrugs his bony shoulders. "Am I wrong?"

He is not wrong. Babushka would hate that I do not play. She would hate that I cannot think of her and smile.

"I wish I make you meet her," I tell Brandon. "She like the way in that faculty-student game you jump so high to make every rebound."

"Thanks," he says. And then he smiles. "My mom used to say I could touch the sky."

"You are her star."

He looks at me. "I told you she called me that?"

"No."

"Well," he says. "Well."

Perhaps I do bad on the ESP test. But I always do know — Brandon is a star.

conclusion
brandon kelly

MY GRANDMA ASKED ME THE OTHER DAY IF I'M STILL mad she made me do this stupid science project. I told her I'm richer. My foul shot's better. I guess I'm not mad.

Thing is, when Marina's grandma died it made me super mad. Marina's a nice girl and all, but right then I wished I never met her. I don't care how much my foul shot improved.

I didn't want to hear about dying. I didn't want to hear Grandma say those words again. There wasn't so much difference between the library, you know, and Mercy Hospital. Plastic chairs your legs stuck to, janitor mopping the halls, cafeteria smell in the air. People all around but oh so quiet.

It was like going back in time. And don't try and tell me that's not supernatural.

Marina says her grandma died of a closed-up heart. Maybe she meant heart attack and got her words messed up. That's really what a heart attack is, you know, when your arteries get all hard and close up. You don't get any blood to your heart and it just stops. Ma told me that once.

But I had this flash of intuition that Marina meant about how her grandma was always thinking of Russia and wanting to go back and feeling sad inside her heart, because things here were so different and all.

I can see how that could kill a person.

If I could go back, I would. Back to Baltimore, back to two years ago. Seems like all I can think about sometimes.

I wish Michael could believe in the Tooth Fairy till he's eighty. I wish he could grow up thinking somebody's always going to take care of him and love him, and do magic to take away the hurt. Michael's seven years old, and he already knows there's no Tooth Fairy.

Ma was the Tooth Fairy. I wonder if Darius knows he's supposed to take care of that now.

My heart feels hard when I think about it, and sometimes I get these pains. Right where I think my heart must be. I wonder if that's how Marina's grandma felt before she died.

I talked to my grandma about it. She's getting up there, and maybe her heart isn't so good. I worry that maybe she's going to leave us, too.

I asked her, does she get those heart pains like I do?

She said yeah. She does. She does get them sometimes when she thinks about Ma. But it hurts less and less these days. Once in a while she can think about her and it doesn't hurt even a little.

Grandma's good and strong. She says I shouldn't worry. She'll be around a long while yet.

To be on the safe side, I asked Claire the psychic about

that. You know what Claire said? She said Grandma's right. We've got lots of time ahead of us. Good times, too, Claire says.

Sometimes I don't think that can be. But then I'll be outside on the court. It's so cold, colder than the day Ma died.

"Cold?" Marina laughs at me. "In Russia this is like the springtime."

No freaking way, I tell her. What did Babushka think was so great about Russia, anyhow?

Me and Marina start playing and sure enough, we get warm real fast. Our hearts are pumping that blood good.

And that little chest pain, the one you get from breathing in the freezing air—pretty soon it does go away.

conclusion
ben lloyd

WE HAVE DEFINED ESP AS THE PROCESS OF ACCUMU-
lating knowledge that cannot be gained through the use of
our five known senses.

When we attempted to crack the lottery, careful scientific
methodology was unsuccessful — although, given ample
time, I am confident it would have worked. Meanwhile, hap-
hazard guessing led to a $500 jackpot. Was this a coinci-
dence? Or were other forces at work?

When Claire drew pictures formed in Kathleen's mind
with no assistance from the five known senses, the probability of coincidence decreased significantly. However, the un-
expected appearance of said results remains to be explained.

It would seem that interpretation of these findings re-
quires intellectual reserves of a paranormal nature. Failing
these, one must fall back on intuition.

My mother says that without intuition, scientists might
not have stumbled upon nuclear physics, cellular biology,
or modern medicine.

I recently read a biography of Marie Curie, and I see that she may have a point.

My mother has read this same biography.

We talk about books and reading and writing. We talk about reporting, which starts with a question—just like science.

We have conversations that my intuition would have said were not possible.

As a scientist, I resolve to hone my intuition.

I'm thinking of asking Claire to help me. Are you reading this, Claire?

conclusion

kathleen phelps

(as told to Claire Phelps)

WE BELIEVE IN ESP. WE THINK YOU KNOW WHY. THIS is the funnest project we ever did. Mr. Ennis is the best teacher we ever had. We are a pair of normal sisters again. We can't wait till next year.

conclusion
claire phelps

WATCH MARINA AND BRANDON ON THE BASKETBALL court. The more they practice, the more they know what the other person will do. They don't have to talk; usually they don't even have to look.

Who says telepathy is an "extra" sense?

For twelve years, Kat and I never tried to see things through each other's eyes. And we didn't.

Now Ji and I have stopped trying. And we don't.

Kathleen and I *are* like other sisters. We are like other friends, in the most important way. We need each other.

That doesn't mean things are great between us — or even good most of the time. But we are trying.

What if I'd wound up in the origami club like I originally planned? Somehow Mr. Ennis knew we belonged in Mad Science. Maybe we should give him a Zener card test someday.

sources
benjamin d. lloyd

Bender, David L., and Bruno Leone, ed. *Paranormal Phenomena: Opposing Viewpoints*. San Diego: Greenhaven Press, 1991.

Cassill, Kay. *Twins: Nature's Amazing Mystery*. New York: Atheneum, 1984.

Cobb, Vicki. *Chemically Active! Experiments You Can Do at Home*. New York: J. B. Lippincott, 1985.

Deem, James M. *How to Read Your Mother's Mind*. Boston: Houghton Mifflin, 1994.*

Duncan, Lois, and William Roll, Ph.D. *Psychic Connections: A Journey into the Mysterious World of Psi*. New York: Bantam Doubleday Dell, 1995.

Miller, Kenneth, and Steve Wewerka. "Together Forever." *Life* 19, no. 5, p. 44, 1996.

---

*Despite the (highly) misleading title, an excellent source of information.

Psychic Powers. Alexandria, Va.: Time-Life Books, 1987.

Randi, James. *Flim-Flam! Psychics, ESP, Unicorns, and Other Delusions*. Buffalo: Prometheus Books, 1988.

Van Cleave, Janice. *Janice Van Cleave's Guide to the Best Science Fair Projects*. New York: John Wiley & Sons, 1997.

acknowledgments

THANKS TO OUR MOTHERS, FATHERS, AND GRAND-
parents for assistance with transportation and transcription
and for their helpfulness in general. To Mrs. Gershwin for
keeping things interesting. Special thanks to Grandma/Mrs.
Mathews and Mom/Mrs. Robles for the interest they have
shown in Mad Science as it concerns us. And of course to Mr.
Ennis, a true scientist who can do magic with chemistry.

Thanks also to our friends who were brave enough to take
the Zener card test:

Kamala Roy, Florence Hui, Maritza Delgado, Amy Love,
Tyler Falcone, Cami Rayfield, Jaime Puente, Hosea Whit-
taker, Michael Whittaker, Justin McNamara, Rachael Myers,
Rebecca Schwartz, Alison Ng, Ashleigh Banneker, Ezra Edel-
man, Kate Nelson, Katie Baird, Kaitlynn Neff, Jasmine
Vines, Malaika Young, Christin Colman, Brian Murtaugh,
Jenna VanderVat, Remy St. John, Paul Keegan, and Emily
Sisk-Parrot.

Pizza and ice cream on us when we win the science fair!

JANUARY 13

Clearview Gazette

Science Gone Mad
Mind Games at the Clearview Science Fair
by Ji Eun Oh, Investigative Reporter

Of the thirteen worthy entries in last week's school science fair, there could be only one winner. As Mrs. Mathews announced Friday, this distinction went to Ben Lloyd, Brandon Kelly, Marina Krenina, Claire Phelps, and Kathleen Phelps for their project entitled *Mind Games*. They will go on to compete in the county science fair at Twin Knolls Middle School in February.

The subject of their investigation, ESP, has become a hot topic of late at Clearview Middle School. Teachers must begin their lessons by telling students to put away their Zener cards. Allowance money is spent daily on the lottery (although technically Clearview students are too young to play).

Continued next page

Claire Phelps (who, according to reliable sources, has never demonstrated signs of psychic abilities in the past) issued a terse "no comment" when asked about her strategy for selecting the winning lottery number in conjunction with sister Kathleen.

An independent investigation, however, has revealed the following facts.

On page 111 of the project report, Kathleen Phelps mentions that her sister smells "lemony." This occurs just after an incident where Claire has "telepathically" drawn a picture of a word Kathleen was picturing in her mind.

A review of the sources listed by Ben in the bibliography uncovered an interesting reference. It stated that, when held under a hot lamp, invisible ink made from lemon juice becomes visible.

Upon re-reading Claire's description of the events surrounding the "telepathic" drawings, I realized that use of a lemon juice aid could in fact account for these results. Particularly given the occurrence of the events in Mr. Ennis's classroom, where hot lizard lamps are known to be present.

Mad Science spokesperson Ben Lloyd vehemently denied these allegations, claiming that lemons would certainly appear in the Materials section of the project had they been used.

When pressed for further details, he replied, "Not everyone in the world is a cheater. Don't you know Claire better than that?"

Maybe this reporter does. But opinion is approximately as useful in journalism as it is in science. I am here only to report the facts.

Best wishes, Mad Scientists, in your quest for science fair gold.

Exhibit I

The Waverly Times

February 11

Celebrating Science

Clearview Students Continue Their Winning Ways

by Joanna Robles
Staff Writer

FOUR months after winning the lottery, five Clearview Middle School students have another win to celebrate—first place in the Howard County Science Fair for their research on ESP.

Over pepperoni pizza (purchased for their sponsors with lottery proceeds), the students discussed the significance this project has held in their seventh-grade year.

Marina Krenina, a budding scientist who barely spoke English at the beginning of the school year, is grateful for the friends she has made through the project. "This is the best way to become American," she stresses. "To try to understand how they think. It is—what is the word?"

"Interesting?" suggested several Mad Scientists.

Marina laughed. "Interesting. Yes. I will say that."

Claire Phelps, who selected the winning lottery number along with her twin sister, Kathleen, echoes these sentiments. "That's what our project was about. Understanding other people. Sometimes it works, sometimes it doesn't . . ."

"But it never works if you don't try," Kathleen chimed in, seemingly finishing her twin's thought.

Five of the six initial ESP investigators found themselves in James Ennis's science class last September by unhappy accident. But when the time came to sign up for a second semester, there were five names on the list. (A sixth member left the club several months ago due to personal reasons.)

"I wanted to be in the basketball club before," admitted Brandon Kelly. "But I did learn more from Mad Science. Even about basketball."

The sixth young scientist and unofficial group leader, Benjamin Lloyd, conceded that the project differed considerably from his expectations. "It was pretty cool, though."

Apparently realizing intuitively that his reporter mother would enjoy a bite of butter pecan ice cream, he shared a spoonful with her. "Bet you didn't know science could be this much fun," Lloyd declared.

Dear Mom,
    Please insert state science fair article here.

        Yours truly,
        Ben